Love on Ice

Canon City Series
Book 2

Lauren Marie

Dedication

For all the ladies at Evergreen Romance Writers, I love all your support and helpful hints.

Acknowledgements

Thanks go to Jennifer Conner and the folks at Books to Go, Now, for the opportunity and my editor
for the great editing. It's so great to be working with you. I must always thank Mary Allen at American Gramaphone for all the crazy email questions and answers. I appreciate all the help. Mannheim Steamroller still rocks.
www.mannheimsteamroller.com.
Thank you to my friends and family for their love and support.
Thanks, as always, to my readers, Elizabeth Ainsley and Tiffany Hinnenkamp. You help is always appreciated.

For news and updates, check out laurenmariebooks.com.
Other books by Lauren Marie:
Love's Embers - Canon City Series book 1
Love's Touch - Then and Now
Going to Another Place
and a short story - Book 3 of The Montana Ranch Series - One Touch a Cob's Bar and Grill

ISBN-13:978-1511815666

ISBN-10:1511815663

Let me hold your hand and be your friend.

Let me hold you in my arms and be your lover.

Let me look into your eyes so I know we have forever.

Chapter One

"Tommy, if you don't stop hitting your brother with that stick, I'll have to put you in the penalty box."

"But, Mr. Hager, Sam cross-checked me in the back." The seven-year-old looked up at him.

"That may be, but I didn't see it. I saw you trip him and then hit him with your stick. Play a clean game, Tommy. I don't want to have to suspend you before the season even starts." Jay Hager stood up straight on his skates and blew his whistle. His mite level hockey team of seven, eight and nine-year-olds all turned to him. "Guys, we've only got two more weeks to practice before the season starts. Remember, we're a team and if you hit someone and they get injured, we won't have them for the opener. We're going to be gentlemen out there and teach those other loser players what the word team means. Do you hear me?"

The kids all cheered and tapped their sticks on the ice.

"Good, let's do a couple more skate rounds and then we'll call it a day." Jay blew his whistle and watched the kids move around the rink. "Sam, come here a second," he said to Tommy's brother. The kid skated over and stood in front of him. Jay put a hand on his shoulder. "Listen to me. You're nine years old and you'll probably be moving to the squirts next year, but I need your help. The younger kids need an older skater to look up to and if you and Tommy keep acting out the stuff that goes on at home, I won't be able to make you captain this year. Do you get what I'm saying, Sam?"

"Yeah, I won't cross check Tommy anymore." Sam shifted from skate to skate.

"Good, I'm counting on you. Go finish the practice for me, okay?" Jay looked across the ice at one of his parent assistants who tried to break up a skirmish. Sam skated over to help out and Jay wanted to laugh. Sam would be helpful for about five minutes, but when he started to play again, he'd forget everything Jay said.

After ten minutes, Jay blew his whistle. "Okay, guys. That was a great practice. You look killer out there. Be sure to get lots of rest this week and eat good, not all that junky stuff. I'll see you next week."

He skated off the ice with his team. After he put on his blade guards, he walked to the bleachers where his tennis shoes waited. He saw a strawberry blonde woman, sitting by herself a few rows up and smiled at her. Jay saw her off and on over the last couple of weeks and thought she looked cute. He tried to think of an unusual way to approach her so he wouldn't sound fake or cliché. He hadn't dated or asked anyone out in so long he'd forgotten how to do it, and he couldn't believe how nervous he felt.

He sat down and started to unlace his skates. Sam and Tommy's mom walked up and sat down next to him.

"Hey, Sara. Do Sam and Tommy fight as much at home as they do on the ice?" He leaned over and took off a skate.

"Yeah, a bit. We're thinking about giving Sam his own room. They constantly bicker."

"Sam will be in the squirts next year. Maybe that will help, too. Since they'll be on different teams, hopefully they'll start to develop some loyalty to each other." He finished tying his shoes and picked up his skates.

"Lord, I hope so. Dan has grounded them so many times they'll probably live with us until they're thirty. I'll have him talk to the boys. I'm sorry you have to put up with them."

Jay stood up and patted her on the back. "There's no need to be sorry, Sara. We'll get it worked out. See you next week." He walked through the rink to a set of stairs and went up to his office. He set the skates under his desk and sat down. He heard the music switch on for the figure skating class and sighed.

He'd bought the rink five years before and worked hard to get it turned around. The place was originally a dump, but he'd done a lot of the remodel work himself, hired a couple of employees and did pretty well. The books were in the black which was a relief. They still operated with some open ice hours and Jay hoped eventually there would be more lessons. He'd started the Little Guys hockey league for the kids and really enjoyed coaching.

After he looked at the time sheets for the week and sent them through to his accountant, he got up and poured a cup of coffee from the never-ending pot, which he kept filled all day. He walked out to the balcony area and set his cup on the flat rail. He looked out over the rink and saw the classes going strong. The pre-teen girls were out with their teachers and worked on spins. He looked around the bleachers and saw the strawberry blonde woman still sat with her hands wrapped around a cup. She'd watch the classes and hockey team practices. For some crazy reason, Jay thought he knew her, but couldn't figure out from where. He knew she worked across the road at Harry's Diner, but thought she looked familiar from somewhere else as well.

He picked up his coffee cup and went back down the stairs. He'd tried to catch her last Wednesday, but by the time he'd gotten down to the bleachers she already left the rink.

When he reached the area where she sat, Jay stepped up his pace and casually walked over to the bench where she sat.

She glanced up at him and he saw the most beautiful eyes look into his. They were sky blue, but seemed a bit tinged with purple. He thought she probably wore contacts.

"Hi, I'm Jay Hager. I know this is crazy, but did we go to college together? I went to U.C.B." He sat down next to her.

"Probably not," she said and continued to watch the skaters.

"Are you sure? You really look familiar."

"I didn't go to college, so it's unlikely. I've also never been to Boulder." She sipped from her cup. She didn't look at him and he saw her back straighten as though she'd tensed up. It bugged him a little.

"Do you skate?" He looked at her and saw her eyebrows jump and then crease for just a second.

"Yes."

Jay nodded and thought, *this one doesn't talk much.* "Don't you work over at Harry's?"

"Yes."

"When I saw you in there, I thought I knew you, but I can't figure it out. It isn't from here at the rink. It's one of those things that can drive you nuts at two in the morning."

"Great." She stood up. "It was nice to meet you," she said and started down the bleachers.

Jay sat up straight when he realized she was leaving. She threw her cup in the garbage can and headed to the front. "What's your name?" he called out, but she didn't turn back or answer.

****

Kate Beck crossed the street and walked away from the rink. She followed the street past the diner and looked over her shoulder multiple times to make sure that guy didn't follow. She'd seen him at the rink and in the diner, but had never waited on him. She turned down a driveway and went to the door of the basement apartment she rented. Once inside with the door locked, she exhaled and felt safe. She knew there was no reason to be paranoid, her mother probably gave up the search for her long ago, but she just couldn't be sure. She'd crowned her mother one of the top ten worst sports mothers in the history of the world. She would swear to it on a stack of Bibles.

She'd been on the run for eight years and got very good at covering her tracks. She'd changed her name so many times and found it hard to remember her real name was Stacy Douglas. Her mother hadn't caught up with her for the last three years and in the last year she'd actually let her natural hair color grow out. She still used her alias, Kate Beck. Kathryn was her real middle name and she'd liked Becks music when she used to skate. She'd come up with several aliases since she'd left her mother behind and hoped she could stick with Kate Beck for a while.

She stretched out on the couch that came with the apartment, pulled a blanket over her and then closed her eyes and tried to take a nap. She didn't have to be at work until later and hadn't slept well all the past week.

Her mind turned to the man. She knew he owned the rink and enjoyed watching him coach the kid's hockey team out on the ice. He treated the kids fair and seemed to know a lot about hockey. He wasn't hard on the eyes, either. He was very tall with gorgeous golden-brown eyes. One of the women at the diner, Shar, went to high school with him a few years ago and said she wouldn't have minded dating him at one time, but now felt he was better friend material. Besides, her husband wouldn't go for a threesome. Shar said he once played for an NHL farm team, but messed up his knee really bad.

Kate rolled over onto her side and tried to relax. She wanted to forget everything, but for some reason her brain continued to roll back to Jay. She wanted to forget Stacy Douglas, but the memories always found an inconvenient time to haunt her. She tried to stay in one place for at least six months, but if she started to feel trapped, she'd pack up her bag and leave. Canon City seemed like a nice place to hunker down for the winter, but she'd thought that way in other towns.

About a year ago, the loneliness began to bug her more and more, and she couldn't figure out a way to make it stop. She lived in a small town in

Wyoming then and the winter was very hard. Other than working, she'd spent most of her time in the tiny apartment she'd rented. The loneliness became bad in the middle of the night. Wherever she worked, she never talked to the other employees much. She never shared any fun news -- not that she ever had any fun news. The people she worked with at Harry's Diner were really nice and pleasant. They didn't butt into her business and seemed to accept her as she appeared to them. Shar turned out to be a really good source of information. Kate got all kinds of recommendations about Canon City from the other waitress. Whether it was where to get her hair cut or the location of shops or the library, Shar seemed to know everything.

Kate read any book she could get her hands on, but even that wasn't fun and diverting anymore. When she got to a new town she always went to the library and applied for a card or she went to the used books stores. Lately, she'd been reading romance novels and wondered if she'd ever be able to have a normal relationship with a man. She would really like to wake up in the morning with someone beside her to share the day. She thought about the man at the rink and wondered if he was nice or if he had some weird dark side that never showed up in public.

She moved onto her back and ran her hands through her hair. She needed to stop reading the romance novels. They made her want too much. She frowned and wondered if that was why she'd felt so alone these past months. Was she too stupid to realize that the stories she'd read were just stories and she'd almost certainly never have a happy ending?

Chapter Two

Five o'clock rolled around and Kate put on the stupid pale blue uniform dress she wore for work and her white sneakers. When she arrived at the diner, she dumped her jacket and purse in her locker and went to find out which section she'd work that night. The head waitress pointed and said Kate was behind the counter.

An older couple came in and sat mid-way down. She poured them a cup of coffee and took their order. After a while the dinner crowd started to come in and the counter only had a few stools left.

Kate heard the bell above the door and saw Jay Hager walk in. She looked at his dark hair and incredible eyes, and almost started to laugh. His height was impressive. He waved at Harry, the owner, in the kitchen and then he looked at her. Their eyes locked and she quickly walked to the other end of the counter to check on her customers.

She refilled some coffee cups and passed out a couple of bills, then looked down at the other end. He'd sat down by the senior couple who'd just gotten up to leave. He talked to the man and then seemed to listen and laughed.

She saw Shar, the other waitress, walk past him and heard her say, "Hi, coach."

"Hey, are you behind the counter tonight?" he asked.

"No, I'm doing tables. Kate will be with you in a second. Be patient." She smiled at him and continued to check on her tables.

Kate felt a little jealous that Shar felt so comfortable in a room full of people. She wished she could stay here long enough to learn what that felt like.

After she poured another coffee, Kate got a couple of tickets ready and gave them to the customers. She knew she couldn't ignore the coach and would just have to play it cool. She walked over and took her pad out of her apron pocket. "Can I get you anything to drink?"

He smiled up at her and looked at her name tag. "Yes, Kate. Could I get coffee with some creamer?"

She nodded and went to the coffee pot. She pulled a small cream pitcher out of the half-fridge and walked back to him. She turned a cup over and poured. "Are you ready to order?" She set the pot back on a burner and waited for him to answer.

"What are the specials tonight?"

"Chicken fried steak with mashed potatoes and vegetables, and a mushroom Swiss burger with fries." She waited patiently.

"What about the soup?" He continued to smile at her and she started to get annoyed.

"Cream of broccoli and barley beef."

"Hmm...I think the burger medium-well with French fries sounds good."

She wrote it down. "Thank you, sir." She put the ticket up on the wheel and spun it into the kitchen. Two orders waited and she reached for them. She walked to the end of the counter and delivered them to the customers. She went back half way to the window and looked at the other end of the counter toward the back. The people down there looked happy.

She could feel his eyes watch her as she moved. She wanted to go on a break, but started work less than an hour ago. She shook her head and did her best to ignore him, but then his burger arrived in the pass-through window. She reached for it and took it down to him.

She put the plate down in front of Jay. "Do you want ketchup?"

"Yes, please." He picked up a fry and put it into his mouth. "Harry makes great fries, don't you think?"

Kate reached under the counter and brought up a bottle of ketchup. "Sure," she said and placed the bottle down. She turned and walked away from him.

She took care of the other customers and after a while, put on her good waitress face and walked up to him with the coffee pot. "Can I warm your coffee up?"

He swallowed the last bite of his burger and smiled again. "Yes, thank you. I wondered Kate, if I could buy you a cup of coffee at the rink tomorrow?"

She warmed up his coffee and wanted to get out of the diner. "No, thank you," was all she could get out.

"You are planning to be over there in the morning, aren't you?"

"No, I have to work tomorrow." She turned away and helped another customer.

Just at that time - Kate couldn't believe her luck - Harry walked up to her and in a mid-range voice said, "Since you're off tomorrow, I thought you'd want your pay check."

Kate wanted to crawl under the counter. She

didn't have to turn around to know everyone in the vicinity heard. She felt the heat blaze in her cheeks. "Thank you," she said and put the check into her pocket. She walked to the opposite end of the counter and took her pad out of her pocket. There were three bills to get prepared and one of them was Jay's. She felt so crazy in the head that she'd lied to him, and been caught, that it made her hand shake as she got the bill ready. She took the other two bills to those customers first and then walked down to his station.

Jay looked up at her, but didn't smile. "You could have just said *no.*"

"I did just say *no*. I'm sorry the rest was a lie." She set the ticket next to his cup and started to walk away.

"Kate, you can still watch the classes. I won't bother you," he said and stood up.

She looked up at him and nodded. "Thank you," she said as he turned to go up front to pay his bill.

She watched him leave and the usual little guilt bug that she'd been plagued with for years started to chew at her gut. She didn't know him, but he wore an easy smile. Why should she feel guilty? It was best not to get involved with anyone. She didn't even talk much to the other waitresses or customers. She looked around the diner and suddenly felt very alone. Her part of the planet looked small.

****

Jay drove his Jeep back to his house about ten miles away. When he pulled into the driveway he set the brake and turned the engine off.

He couldn't turn his thoughts away from that woman, Kate, and it pissed him off she'd lied to him. Jay hated that more than getting his teeth worked on, and he'd been lied to more times than he cared to count in the last couple of years by women.

The last woman he'd been involved with could lie and convince him the sun looked blue. She'd played him and it wrecked his trust in humanity for a time. It happened several years ago and he wished he could get over it, but his trust button turned out to be a problem. Did the women he dated hold onto their own histories and use them against him?

He looked out the front windshield and shook his head. She carried herself well with a straight back and her head up, but he saw sadness and fear in her eyes. It grabbed his heart. He still felt like he knew her from somewhere.

Jay opened the Jeep's door and pulled his duffle bag off the passenger seat. After he got into the house, turned the heat up and took his coat off, he went into his office and sat at his desk. His land line flashed. He turned on the speaker, pressed in a code and learned there were five messages. The first two were from his mom. She wanted him to come over for dinner soon. The third from the security man at the rink with nothing that couldn't wait until tomorrow.

The fourth call was from Monica Everett, a mother of a ten-year-old figure skater.

"Hi, Jay. Sorry I missed you. I'll try back later," she said. He hit the erase button. The fifth call was from her again an hour later. "Hi again, Jay. I hoped to touch base with you. I had a really great time two weeks ago and can't understand why you haven't called. I can understand why you'd not want to get involved with someone with a kid. I just don't understand why we couldn't have some fun. I love dancing and think you'd make a great partner out on the dance floor. Anyway, give me a call. Bye."

Jay hit the erase button again and sat behind his desk. He stared at the phone. Monica told him two weeks ago that a bunch of the parents of kids from the rink wanted to get together for dinner to discuss arrangements for a community rummage sale to raise funds for the hockey teams' uniforms. When he'd gotten to the restaurant, she'd been the only parent there and didn't want to discuss anything having to do with kids. She'd made excuses and said he'd probably misunderstood her. When someone says *a group of people are going out to dinner* how is it a misunderstanding? He'd asked himself that question a couple of times and figured she'd lied her way through the evening. He hated liars and wasn't about to become involved with one.

That evening, because of her varied stories, he told her that he wasn't interested. He did find it funny that Monica thought it was because of her daughter. Shelby was a cute, ten-year-old and could be a good little skater if her mom would back off.

Jay turned his computer on with every intention of doing bookkeeping, but got involved with a game - Ice Road to Hell. It wasn't a great game, but it kept him occupied and he didn't have to think about weird women anymore.

Chapter Three

The next week the first signs of fall began to appear. It got darker earlier and the leaves started to turn on some of the trees. The Aspen's started to flutter golden in the afternoon sun.

Kate felt Canon City would be a good place to settle in for the winter and figured if she just kept to herself, everything would be fine. She'd leave town when spring hit anyway, so it didn't really matter.

She decided to stay away from the rink that week and kept to her apartment. She spent a lot of time reading books from a used book store in a strip mall about a mile from where she lived. The current book turned out to be dull and she put it in a bag with several others. She'd make a trip down to the store and get another dozen or so to keep her occupied. She never bought a television. It just wasn't practical to pack up if she needed to leave in a hurry.

On Friday evening, she worked the tables and Jay came into the diner. He sat in her area and she wondered why. She grabbed a small pitcher of cream from the refrigerator and a coffee pot and walked over to his table.

"I know I shouldn't assume, but I thought you might want coffee tonight?" she asked and set the creamer down.

"You remembered. Yeah, coffee's my drink of choice." He smiled.

She turned the cup over and poured coffee. "The specials are turkey pot pie with a garden salad and meatloaf with baked potato and vegetables. The soups are minestrone and chicken noodle," she told him.

Jay laughed. "Thank you. Meatloaf sounds good."

She started to turn away, but he stopped her.

"You haven't been by the rink at all this week. I hope what happened last time I was in here didn't make you uncomfortable," he said.

Kate looked down at the notepad in her hands. "I didn't think it would be a good idea."

"Why not?"

"I didn't want...that is, I thought maybe you'd be uncomfortable if I continued to come in and just sit and watch the skaters. I didn't want to do that."

She shrugged and looked down at him. Jay really had nice, warm brown eyes and she thought for a second how easy it would be to get lost in them. But she knew if she were to get involved with anyone, all of her past baggage would make any man turn away from her. Warm brown eyes were nice to look at, but he'd probably lose interest in her, too.

He sat back on his chair and folded his hands on the table. "Well, I don't have a problem with it, so if you want to come back in, go for it. The coffee stand needs your business."

She nodded and laughed. "Thank you. Let me get your order in." She turned and walked to the counter in a daze. He seemed so kind and she didn't know how to take it.

The bell over the door jingled and she watched a man and woman come in. They looked around and when they saw Jay sat by himself, they walked over and joined him. Kate grabbed two menus and walked over to the table.

"Kate, this is Lark and Charlie Stone. I've known them going on forever. Guys, this is Kate," Jay said and smiled, again.

"Hi, Kate. You're new here," the woman named Lark said. "How long have you been working for Harry?"

"Just a couple of weeks. What can I get you to drink?"

"Coffee's fine. Are you from the area?" the man asked.

"No, I'm new to Canon City. I'll go get the coffee." She moved away from the table and heard Jay say something about *not talking much*. She figured he probably spoke about her, but tried not to get too wound up by it.

Lark and Charlie ordered the meatloaf, too and raved about Harry's cooking. Kate hadn't tried his meatloaf, but according to the three of them, it was the best in town.

After they left, she went to bus the table and found Jay had left her a ten dollar tip, which seemed way too much for a five dollar meal. She didn't complain though and pocketed the money.

Chapter Four

That night, Kate couldn't sleep. When she did doze off she got hit with a really bad dream. Her mother screamed at her about being an ungrateful bitch and wanting too much. Her platinum hair shone so bright, that Kate couldn't see anything and then her mother slapped her across the face. When she woke up, tears rolled out of her eyes and she got out of bed.

In the bathroom, she rinsed her face and leaned over the sink. She'd sworn years ago she would never cry about her past again, but whenever these dreams occurred she weakened and the tears flowed. She hated that she let this happen and tried to control her emotions.

Kate walked into the living room, and thought about reading for a while. She looked at the clock on the wall and saw it was seven-thirty on a Saturday morning. She decided to get dressed and go for a walk. The traffic wouldn't be too bad yet and it still would be nice and quiet. She put on a sweater and jeans, and laced her sneakers up. She made her way around the neighborhood and found the trail she'd followed several times before. It went toward a stream bed, up into another neighborhood and came out on the main road that would take her back to the diner and her street.

Morning was her favorite time of day. She didn't mind working nights and would happily give up some sleep to watch the sun rise, although she'd missed it this morning. Canon City was a nice town, surrounded by mountains, trees and blue sky. Kate thought she could be comfortable here, but knew the time would come when the need to move on would come over her. It would settle in her bones until she did just that. She'd run for eight long years already and it'd become second nature.

At eight-thirty, she stood on the corner by the diner, which was open for breakfast. She knew the coffee cart would be open at the ice rink and couldn't decide if she wanted to talk to the people she worked with or watch the little kids as they practiced with their coaches. She decided she didn't really want to talk to anyone and headed for the rink.

There were a couple of moms ahead of her in the coffee line. She waited patiently and looked around the rink. To her right, sat a long skate rental counter and she saw the cashier hand a pair of skates over to a young girl who wore a skating outfit. She handed a twenty dollar bill up to him and walked away. Kate saw the guy stuff the money into his pocket.

She kept an eye on him and the next kid to come up was accompanied by her mom. The woman handed the cashier a credit card and he rang it up on the register. The woman signed and walked away. A few seconds later, another kid walked up with cash and the guy didn't ring up the rental. Kate knew what he was doing.

"Excuse me, miss. Can I help you?"

She looked at the teenager who ran the coffee cart and smiled. "Sorry, Americana tall, please."

Kate took her coffee to the bleachers and sat down. She warmed her hands with the cup and watched the youngsters out on the ice. She thought about the cashier at the rental counter and wondered what she should do. She knew he skimmed the cash from those kids. Jay seemed like a nice enough guy and she figured she should tell him what his employee was up to. It happened at restaurants she'd worked in over the years, employees stole cash from the registers. She'd never gotten involved before, and always felt guilty about not saying a word.

She looked around the arena and saw Jay off with a group of boys at the end of the ice. The kids were getting their skates on and prepared for their practice session.

She sighed, stood up and walked toward the group. As she got closer, she could hear him give his boys a pep talk. She stood by the rail and waited. One of the kids spotted her and tapped Jay on his arm.

"Mr. Hager, I think that lady wants to talk to you," the kid said and pointed at her.

Jay turned around and she saw a crease form between his eyebrows. She smiled a little and nodded.

"I just need a minute," Kate said.

"You guys get warmed up. We have a half hour before we're on the ice, so stretch it out good." He turned to her and motioned away from the kids with his hand.

She followed him to a set of benches and he turned to face her. "I just thought you'd want to know the guy at the skate rental counter is ripping you off." She saw his eyes glance past her to the counter and then back. "I've seen it before. On some of the cash charges he doesn't ring them up and pockets the cash. I feel like a tattle-tail, but while I waited in line for coffee he did it five or six times."

"He's only been here a couple of months, but I wondered why the charges were going down over there." He put his hand under her elbow and led her to a stairwell. "Come with me."

They went up to the balcony level and when they got to a cross hallway he turned left. They looked over the edge of the railing and after a few minutes, they saw the guy do it again.

"Damn. Would you stay right here for a second? I'll be back."

"Okay." She watched him walk back to the stairs and heard his footfalls go down. She looked over the edge of the balcony and saw him head to the rental counter. He said something to the guy, who then followed Jay back to the stairs.

Kate heard his voice as they came up, but they must have turned down the other hallway. She tip-toed to the door for this section and could hear Jay ask the guy to empty his front pockets. The guy refused, but apparently was convinced to change his mind. Jay fired him and told him to get his ass off the property before he called the sheriff.

After a few minutes, Jay reappeared and they watched the crook leave the rink.

"That was nice of you to not call the cops," she said and looked out at the skaters.

"You wouldn't by chance need another job?"

"No, I'm busy enough."

Jay nodded and smiled. "See, now you have to let me buy you lunch."

"I think your offer was only for a cup of coffee." She looked up at him.

"Hey, you just saved my bacon from getting ripped off anymore. I'll tell the coffee cart you get free drinks for life. You're my heroine and deserve more than coffee, which you seem to have anyway."

"It doesn't take much to impress you, does it?"

Jay leaned on the rail and crossed his arms. "Meet me back here at eleven-thirty?" he asked.

She looked up at him. "Today? I don't know. I need to get some sleep and..."

"Aren't you off work today?" He glanced at her with an eyebrow raised.

"No, I really have to work tonight." She laughed.

"You do need to eat before you go to work, right?"

She looked at him, again and felt warmth flood her chest. "Okay." She turned and started down the stairs. She tossed her coffee cup in a garbage receptacle and left the building. She raged at herself all the way back to her apartment. *Why did she agree to have lunch with this guy? Had she lost her mind?*

She stood in the living-room for several minutes and tried not to hyperventilate. She hadn't experienced a panic attack for a couple of years. Her brain yelled at her in a non-stop diatribe and she worked very hard to shut it up. One lunch with a stranger couldn't cause any trouble. He didn't know who she was, so there wasn't a chance he'd be in touch with her mother.

"Idiot, it's just lunch. Get your shit together and it will be over in no time," she mumbled to herself and went into the bedroom.

Kate looked at the few pieces of clothing that hung sadly in the closet. She decided to take a shower and then wear the one decent pair of jeans she owned. What she'd wear on top was a whole issue of its own.

She let the hot water pound on her head and tried to figure out why she felt so nervous. She'd spent the last eight years staying away from relationships of any kind. Wherever she chose to crash land she didn't get close to the people she worked with. What was it about this guy that made her agree to have lunch? She didn't have an answer and hoped it was more than his brown eyes.

She dried her hair and put on a little make-up and then stood and stared at the closet again with her arms crossed over her chest. She finally went to the bureau, and pulled out her purple fleece turtle neck. She put on the jeans and grabbed a grey knit vest.

She looked at the clock by her bed and she saw it was only ten. "Great, I have an hour and a half to go insane. Just peachy." She went out to the living room, sat on the couch and picked up her book.

****

Jay felt excited that Kate accepted his invite. In the past, if someone lied to him, it was difficult for him to forgive. There was something about this woman, though, that made him want to know more. She held a mystery in her eyes, which he found so beautiful. He still wondered if she wore contacts, though. And she'd caught his cashier stealing the cash from his till. That felt like a good way to reprieve herself in his eyes. Her lie wasn't much compared to what she'd done for him.

After the kids finished their practice, he raced up to his office and got cleaned up. There was a black flannel shirt that hung from a coat stand and he decided, after he dusted it off, to put it on. He tucked it in and grabbed his coat.

He went back down the stairs and over to the rental counter. "Hey, Jerry. Thanks for covering today. I'll get the job posted first thing. Can you come in tomorrow for a few hours?"

"Sure, coach, no problem. I can always use the extra bucks," Jerry said. He was a great seventeen-year-old high school kid, who worked off and on at the rink. He'd played on one of the peewee teams a few years back and Jay knew he could trust the kid. It was a relief to know the till wouldn't be robbed anymore.

Jay turned around and looked out at the rink. When he started to turn back to the counter, he saw Kate walk in through the front doors. He almost didn't recognize her with her hair down. She looked beautiful and he felt himself pump up a little with excitement. He waved and met her half way by the benches.

"Hi, you look great," he said and smiled.

"Thank you."

He could tell she was a bit nervous and thought that was good since he was, too. "Have you decided where you'd like to have lunch?"

"I've only been in Canon City about a month. Other than McDonald's and the diner I don't know any other restaurants."

"What kind of food do you like?" He moved toward the door and watched her walk next to him.

"I'll eat pretty much anything. I'm not big on over-stuffed sandwiches, though."

Jay felt a hand on his arm and stopped. He looked to his right and saw Monica, the woman who kept leaving him messages and was a known pain-in-the-ass liar.

"Excuse me, Jay. Do you have a minute?"

"Actually, we're just heading out. Can we talk later?" Jay pulled his arm away from her and almost started to laugh when his mind turned to cooties. It was good to know that even though he was twenty-nine years old he could still think like a kid.

"This will only take a minute. I'm sure your friend won't mind."

He saw Monica give Kate a look and didn't like it. He turned to Kate and sighed. "I'll be right back." She nodded and he saw her eyes squint at Monica.

They moved away and she turned to look up at him. "Who's your new friend, Jay?"

He didn't like the tone of her voice. "Doesn't Shelby have a lesson this morning?" he asked and tried to keep it light.

"Yes, she's on the ice now. I'm just wondering if you got any of my messages?" She moved closer to him.

"Yeah, I did."

"Why didn't you call back?"

"Look, Monica, if I gave you the wrong impression at that dinner, when I said I wasn't interested, then I apologize." Jay took a step back from her. "I'm not interested in dating you and can only think of you as someone I went with to high school. It has nothing to do with Shelby. She's a great kid and I think you should focus on her." He tried to move away from her, but she stepped in front of him and put her hand on his chest.

"Are you saying I'm a bad mother?" She frowned.

"No, I didn't say that. I just don't think we have very much in common and you'd get pretty bored with me." He moved around her and smiled at Kate. He appreciated her patience.

"Jay, how can you say that when you won't even give me a chance?" She grabbed his arm again.

He turned to her and wrapped his free hand around her wrist. He held it tight and felt like pushing her away. "Monica, you bamboozled me into thinking I'm going to a group dinner and tried very unsuccessfully to seduce me. I'm not interested and think we should put that night behind us." He pushed her hand away and took a step back.

"So, I suppose you're sleeping with her." She turned her angry gaze to Kate. "I can offer you so much more, Jay. Please, just give me a chance," Monica begged.

"Yeah, you can lie with the best of them. The answer is no, Monica. You have nothing I'm interested in getting to know." Jay walked over to Kate. "Sorry about that, let's get out of here." He looked over his shoulder at Monica, who wore a deep frown on her face. He hoped that would be the end of it with her.

.

Chapter Five

They walked out of the ice rink building and Kate followed him to a dark blue Jeep. Jay opened the door for her and helped her up to the seat. While she closed the door, he ran around the vehicle and plunked himself into the driver's seat. "There's a place that serves all kinds of burgers, soups and salads. That kind of stuff. It's up at the Gorge. It's a brewing company and they have their own beers. Do you like beer?" He started the engine.

"Beer is fine, but since I have to work tonight I'll probably just have coffee."

Jay pulled out onto the highway. He noticed her fingers were laced together tightly and her knuckles turned white. He needed to think of a way to get her to relax. "Where are you from, Kate?"

She turned her head to look at him. "I'm pretty much from all over the place."

"Was your family military?"

"No, not military." She stared ahead out the

front window. "I was born in Portland, Oregon. Are you from Canon City?"

"Yep, born and raised. A long time ago, I was with a junior hockey team up in Washington State. We played a few times down in Portland. It seemed like a nice town."

"How come you don't play anymore?"

"I banged my knee up pretty bad when I was nineteen. A few surgeries later the team released me and no matter how hard I worked, I couldn't get the strength back."

"How long have you owned the rink?"

"About five years."

"It looks like good, hard ice. You've done a good job with it."

"Hard ice? How do you know about types of ice?"

"I don't know, I must have read it somewhere," she said.

He nodded and watched the road. "Well, hopefully, now, since you busted my thief, I'll have a little more money on the books. Lunch isn't really enough to thank you. You said you skate. How about some free ice time." He smiled at her.

"That's not necessary. I haven't skated for a long time, but thank you. How long have you coached the kid's team?"

Jay did most of the talking on their way to the brewery. He thought it was funny how she kept the focus of the conversation on him, but at least she talked.

****

They ordered their meals and Kate sipped her coffee. She thought Jay worked very hard to make her feel comfortable and it did give her a relaxed moment but she flipped that switch off quickly. She didn't know how long she would stay in Canon City and didn't want to hurt anyone along the way.

"So, Kate, if your family wasn't military, why did you move 'round so much?" he asked.

Kate felt frozen for a second, unsure how to answer him. "It was jobs, mostly." She looked into her coffee cup. "I mean, it wasn't my family that moved, it was me and I moved to find jobs."

"Why?"

She looked at him and didn't know what to say that didn't make her sound like an idiot. "I know you don't like lying and I don't want to lie to you, but...I'd rather not talk about it."

She watched him sit back in his chair and take a sip of his beer. The litany about her being nuts for accepting his lunch invite, started in her head again. Jay seemed really nice and, of course, he wanted her information, but there was so much she wouldn't ever talk about. It became difficult to tell him anything.

"Where do I know you from? It's going to drive me crazy, but I've seen you before," he said.

"I don't think we've ever met. I've never been to a hockey game and this is my first time in Canon City. Maybe it was in another life or something."

He laughed. "Okay, why do you hang out at skating rinks? You're not watching the kids for some evil reason?" He grinned at her.

She knew he was teasing, but felt her eyebrows pull down. "No, no perverted reason, I promise. It's just fun to watch them learn new moves. There are times I want to strangle the coaches and parents, but it's none of my business, so I just watch."

"I hear you on that parent thing. They can be a pain. Have you ever taught skating?"

She looked at him. "No. You're a good coach with your hockey team."

"You think so?" He smiled.

"Yeah, you're very patient with the kids and don't make them feel like they're stupid. There are two boys that seem to always be fighting, though."

"Sam and Tommy. They're brothers and haven't accepted each other yet. It's high competition time around those two. Next year Sam, he's the older boy, may move up to the squirt division and I think it will help."

They ate lunch and when they were finished went out to the Jeep. Jay pulled the vehicle onto the highway heading into the mountains.

"I should get back soon. I have to get ready for work," Kate said and felt a little uneasy about the direction they were headed.

"We're not going far. I want to show you something incredible, since you're new to the area and all. I'd like to give you a little tour," he said.

They drove for about ten minutes and came to a large public parking lot. When they got out of the Jeep, Jay held his hand out with a smile.

"I'd ask you to close your eyes, but it might be a little soon for that."

They walked side by side on a dirt path. Kate felt uneasy to hold his hand and couldn't think about or see anything around her. Jay's fingers were very warm and for some crazy reason she couldn't define, it made her feel safe, but she knew it was wrong. She didn't want to give him any ideas about any involvement. It couldn't happen with them and she hoped he could understand that.

They walked around a corner and Kate's jaw dropped open. "Oh my God..."

"This is a tourist trap, but I love the view of the gorge. During the week when people are at work it can be really quiet out here. Do you want to walk out on the bridge?" He pointed to his right.

Kate followed his finger. She made a funny squeak sound and found she couldn't form words. She looked up at him and nodded.

They followed another path and walked out onto a pedestrian-only bridge. The sign said they were over a thousand feet up and it was the highest bridge in the United States. She looked over both sides and when they were about a third of the way out, she stopped. She moved to the rail and looked over the side. Other people moved across the bridge and kids charged around making a lot of noise.

"Is that the Arkansas River?" she asked.

"Yep."

"I've seen the ads for river rafting," she said and looked straight down at the river.

"Have you ever been rafting?"

"No, but it looks fun."

"It can be. They have zip-lines, too. That can be a kick."

Kate straightened up and looked up at the sky. She realized that Jay had put his arm around her waist and she stepped away from him. It would have been nice to feel his arms around her, but her head kept telling her it was all wrong. She glanced up and saw he looked down at her with a bit of a frown on his lips. Their eyes locked and Kate became tongue-tied again.

"Kate, you have no reason to be afraid of me," he said and touched her cheek.

"I'm not afraid of you."

"Why did you just start to shake like a leaf?" He ran his thumb over her lips and moved a step closer to her.

"Fear of heights?" She closed her eyes as his lips came down and gently touched hers. He moved his tongue along her lip line and she felt him adjust his body around so they were face to face. He put his other arm around her and his lips pressed down harder. His tongue slowly traced around the inside of her mouth. She felt a warm passion flow into her and it slid down to her pelvis and legs. For a moment, all the voices in her head went quiet and she liked the way his kiss made her feel.

Kate moved her hand up his side and put her palm on his chest. She'd every intention of stepping back, but found her hand gripped his jacket. She did finally pull back and kept her head down for a moment and when she looked up at him, she smiled.

"Thank you, that was nice."

Jay ran his hand through her hair. "Don't be afraid of me. I promise not to hurt you."

Kate pulled out of his arms and started back the way they'd come. She crossed her arms and looked back at him. "I do have to get ready for work. We need to go back."

She wished she didn't feel as though she needed to run back, pack up her duffle bag and hit the road. It wasn't that he scared her. She knew what the main fear in her heart told her. If he figured out who she really was, would he even want to be with her anymore. She'd spent all her life with this fear and she could still hear her mother's voice, *No one will ever want you. If you think otherwise then you're still the stupid kid you've always been.* Her mother said things like that to her over and over until she was seventeen and Kate couldn't get it to stop repeating in her head. It was like a recording that ran in circles. She held a lot of baggage in her head and didn't want to unload it on him.

They drove back to Canon City in silence. She looked out the side window and kept her hands clasped together. She gave Jay the directions to the neighborhood where she lived and he pulled up to the sidewalk outside of the house.

"Thank you for lunch," she said and started to open the door, but he reached across her and held it closed. He looked into her eyes.

"I'm not sure what happened up on the bridge. For a second there I thought maybe I might have a chance with you. I would like to see you again. What time do you get off work tonight?"

"It's usually really late, midnight or one o'clock and I'm pretty tired after a shift." Part of her wanted to meet him and the other part said *no, bad idea, don't go there.* It made her want to scream at the voices to shut up and leave her alone for once. But that was her problem; she didn't want to be alone anymore. She felt so confused.

"That's not too late. Why don't you come over to the rink? I'll get some good skates out and we'll have a skate around. You said you do know how to skate, right? It will be just us on the ice, so if you fall I'll be the only one there to see you and I'll be more than happy to give you a hand to get back up. What size do you wear?"

"Yeah, I do know how and I have my own skates, but it's not...I'm..." She took in a breath and let it out slowly and tried to calm down. "I just..." She looked at his brown eyes and saw something she didn't recognize.

She felt his hand on her cheek and warmth spread through her again. She felt safe and couldn't decide if it was good or not.

"Kate, I have no expectations. I'll leave the front door open and if you want to skate, let yourself in and bring your skates. No one but you and I will be there. If you aren't there by two o'clock, I'll figure I struck out and that will be okay."

"I'll think about it," she whispered.

He brushed his lips over hers and she could feel his warm breath on her face. She turned away and opened the door. She nearly killed herself when she got out and tripped over the sidewalk. She walked with quick steps to the side of the house and didn't look back.

Chapter Six

Jay worked behind the rental counter during the evening. He tried not to think about Kate, but found it difficult. He felt something haunted her and hoped he could find a way around it. He wanted to spend more time with her. Jay couldn't say what it was he found attractive about the woman, but knew her eyes killed him. The bluish-purple mesmerized him and whenever she looked at him, he wanted to melt.

He asked his security guard, Zack, who doubled as the Zamboni driver, to clean the ice after Jay closed the rink and then gave him the night off.

If Kate didn't show up Jay didn't relish the idea of staying overnight at the rink, but he'd done it in the past and could do it again. He started to think that maybe a bottle of wine and some flowers would be nice and would maybe impress her a little, but scratched the idea in case she didn't show up or drink wine.

The time crawled slowly by and at eleven o'clock he heard the engine on the Zamboni fire up. He watched Zack steer the machine out onto the rink and begin the circle. Jay cleaned up the locker rooms and carried the garbage out to the dumpsters behind the building. He walked to the front of the rink carrying a newspaper and a cup of coffee. Zack finished and drove the huge machine out the gate at the other end of the ice.

Jay sat down at one of the tables and thought about looking at the paper, but couldn't concentrate. He wanted to be excited about Kate maybe coming over to the rink, but felt nervous. A couple of times this afternoon when they were at lunch and at the bridge, she'd gotten a frightened look on her face and the last thing he wanted to do was scare her. That kiss out on the bridge rang his bell and he hoped he could convince her to give him a chance.

"Hey boss," Zack called out. Jay looked across the ice and waved. "I'm out of here. Thanks for the night off. The wife waited up for me. Do you want me to lock the doors?"

"No. Leave it open, I'm expecting someone." He watched Zack leave the building and thought of some things he could do to improve the atmosphere. He jumped up and ran for the stairs. He went up to the sound booth and picked a couple of CD's out of the racks that he thought would be good for a skate around. He dimmed some of the lights, but left them on at the front door. He didn't want her to think the rink was closed.

He once again tried to read the paper, but it didn't work and he decided to re-string a bunch of the rental skates. He was putting them back on the shelves when he heard a quiet voice.

"Hi, Jay."

He turned and smiled. "You came over, great." He was both relieved and excited at the same time.

She held a box in her arms and walked to the table where his empty coffee cup sat. She put the box down and took her coat off. Jay realized he stared at her from the counter and moved around it. He walked up to her and still smiled.

"Kate, do you want a bottle of water or pop? I have a new pot of coffee, too. We have both hot and cold."

"Water's fine, thank you." She smiled.

He ran over to the concession stand and grabbed a bottle of water from the refrigerator. When he headed back he saw her look out at the ice. He set the bottle down. "What do you think? Are you ready to give it a try?"

She looked up at him. "It's been a few years. I'll either split my pants or pull something." She sat down and took a Scrunchy off her wrist. She pulled her hair back into a ponytail.

Jay watched her and said, "Oh, oh, hair's going up. This is serious."

"No, it's not serious. I just don't want my hair to fly around my face." She bent over her feet and took off her sneakers. Sitting back up straight, she looked at him. "You were planning to skate tonight, too?"

"Yes, yes I am." He sat down and took off his shoes. "I hope you don't mind hockey skates."

"They'll be on your feet, so, no problem." She opened the box and pulled one of the skates out. The laces were stuffed into the boot and as she took them out, the blade guard fell off.

He glanced over and was surprised. "Wow, those are nice. Where do you get the blades sharpened?"

"I don't remember. It's been a while since they've been out of the box." She put the guard back on and leaned over to put it on her foot. She did the same with the other skate and tightened the laces. She stood up and bounced a little on the blades. She looked down at him. "If I fall on my butt a lot you have to promise you won't laugh your head off."

"No, ma'am. I'd never laugh at you on your butt." He smiled and arched an eyebrow.

"Ha, ha."

Jay watched her walk toward the entrance to the ice. She knelt down and put her hand on the frozen surface, moving it over the ice. He could see her lips move and then she patted the ice. This little ceremony that she did looked familiar and he thought he remembered where he knew her from, but something just didn't add up.

She stood up, removed the blade guards and slid out. He stood up and walked over to the rail. He watched her flow over the clean surface and couldn't believe how smooth and graceful her moves were. He remembered where he knew her from and couldn't believe his luck. The only problem was her name. Kate Beck wasn't the name he remembered.

She stopped mid-ice and turned. "Are you going to skate or not?" she asked.

"Yeah, sorry." He took his guards off, set them next to hers and stepped onto the ice. "Where did you learn to skate?"

"In Portland."

"You're very smooth." He approached her and circled around.

"You have good ice. It's not mushy." She turned and started to glide the rest of the length of the rink.

"What was the kneeling thing you did?" He moved up alongside of her.

"I used to have a friend who said that I should always make friends with the ice before I went out on it. He was Arapaho and I always said the prayer before I'd skate." She turned and started to move backwards.

"Did it help?"

"Sometimes."

"You said *he* told you. Was he someone you were close to?"

"Hmm...we were good friends and I think we were nine or ten years old."

Jay nodded and watched her continue to move backwards. "That's wise for someone so young. We probably should have warmed up."

"For just a skate around? No, we'll be okay." She stopped and looked up at him. "There is something I should say though."

Jay leaned against the boards and waited patiently.

"Our kiss this afternoon was very nice, but..."

"No, no, no buts. The only butts out here tonight are the ones God put right here." He smacked his rear end.

She smiled and then frowned. "I'm not a very good catch, Jay."

"Now, why do you say that?"

"I'm not experienced with good relationships and I have a lot of baggage. I wouldn't want to load you down with it. You seem like a great guy, but I don't want to burden anyone with my history."

"We all carry around loads of bad memories. I'm still pissed at the guy who helped me mess up my knee."

"Well, my bad memories are more than I can take sometimes and I ignore it as much as I can. If it feels like it's getting too close, I pack up my bag and hit the road."

"So that's why you've moved around so much. Maybe it would help if you shared it with someone. Like me, for instance."

"No, it wouldn't help," she said quietly and turned. "It's nice of you to offer, but I wouldn't want to give you the wrong impression and, as I said, you don't need to be burdened with my crap. I do tend to leave a place pretty quick if things don't feel right and I wouldn't want to hurt you in the process."

Jay watched her skate down the ice away from him. She picked up speed and toward the other end of the rink went into a spread eagle, came around to face forward and stepped into a triple axel. His mouth hung open. "How did you do that? That was a great axel."

****

When Kate landed that jump she wanted to whoop for joy and weep at the same time. She hadn't done it for a couple of years, and it felt so good to know that the jump that caused her downfall was still in her arsenal of jumps. She skated backwards and then swung around into a death drop, and then a camel spin. She slowly straightened up into a scratch spin and stopped. She looked down the ice at Jay and heard her mother say she just showed off and no one is impressed with her abilities. She suddenly felt embarrassed and slowly made her way down to where he stood.

"I thought we were skating tonight? You keep leaning against the boards and your mouth is hanging open."

He looked at her and smiled. "That was incredible. How did you do a triple axel? And that death drop. Wow."

She crossed her arms and circled around him. "How is it, a guy who played hockey knows the names of figure skating moves?"

"Ah that, right." He started to move around with her. "See when athletes aren't playing their sport there is a lot of down time with nothing to do. I'm not sure what city we were in, but I started channel surfing on the TV at a hotel where we stayed. Some of the guys watched daytime soap operas. General Hospital was a favorite. I couldn't stand that stuff and on one of the sports networks I got to watch the National championships and later caught the Worlds. I really liked to watch the women skate. They were hot. I just caught on to the jump lingo and other stuff. Can you do a Biellmann?"

"Not anymore. I haven't skated enough and lost the dexterity to do that spin." She couldn't believe the words coming out of his mouth. It impressed her that he even had a clue what a Biellmann looked like and could name a jump she'd just done.

"Did you ever skate in the Nationals?"

Kate suddenly realized she danced on the edge and was getting too comfortable. She didn't want to go there. "No." It felt like only a partial lie and if he found out the truth, hopefully he'd understand, but she wasn't about to tell him what happened to her at Nationals.

"Why not? You are great, even though you haven't skated for awhile. I suppose it's like riding a bicycle. It's something you never forget. Why didn't you skate in the Nationals?"

This was not a discussion she wanted to continue. She turned away from him and headed to the entrance. She picked up her blade guards and stared at them. Jay slid up next to her.

Kate looked up at him. "Lost dreams, nothing but lost dreams." She shrugged and bent over to put the guards on her blades. She straightened up and looked at him.

"I bet it's a long story. I have the time," he said and took her hand.

She stared at their hands and then pulled hers away. She backed up a step. "I should go." She walked around him and off the ice. She tried to figure out why she let him see her skate. She'd never done it before and she knew he might be smart enough to put two and two together. She sat at the table and unlaced her skates.

"Kate, wait a minute." He came over and started untying his own skates. "Listen, I get that you have a history that bugs you and it would be great if you'd let me help, but I won't be pushy. Nosey, yes, but you can tell me or not. I like you and hope we can spend some time together."

She tied the laces on her shoes and put her skates back in the box. This guy made it difficult for her to think and she became so confused. She thought he might be someone who'd listen and not judge her, but she didn't know if she could trust him. They'd only really known each other since this morning. Jay used the two H words, hope and help. She hadn't heard those words in a long time.

"Do you know how to play Broom Ball?" he asked.

She looked up at him. "What?" Her brain found it difficult to sort the question from the confusion in her brain.

"Broom Ball. It's played with sawed-off brooms and a rubber ball about the size of a cantaloupe. It's sort of like hockey," he said.

"No, I've never played."

"I know you're off work on Monday's and it just so happens there will be a game here tomorrow night...wait, I mean tonight. Now I'm confused. It's Sunday now, right?" He shook his head. "Anyway, it starts around six in the evening. It's a bunch of jerks I went to high school with and their girlfriends and wives. Lark and Charlie will be here. You met them at the diner. Sometimes kids come along and play, but this week is adults only. We're serving beer. What do you say? We could have dinner after."

"I don't know." She felt completely flummoxed. She felt like she'd run in two different directions.

"Think about it. I'll give you a lift home tonight." He stood and plucked his jacket from a chair.

"Jay, I only live two blocks from here. I can walk it."

"Nope, won't happen tonight. I'd be a terrible date if I let you walk alone and some jerk tried to attack you. It would be wrong of me to let that happen."

"I understand this is a pretty safe neighborhood and this isn't really a date." She watched as he put on his coat.

"Sure it's a date. We ate food earlier and...well, this isn't like going to the movies, but it is a date."

"You're not going to give in, right?" She laughed.

"Right." He held out his hand.

She looked at him and continued to laugh. "I have to carry my box." She picked it up in both hands and stood. He tried to take it away from her, but she said no. She could carry them just fine.

They got into his Jeep and Kate sat with the box on her lap. She watched him from the corner of her eye. He stopped by the sidewalk in front of the house and pulled the brake on. He turned to her and put his hand on her cheek. She felt warmth come from his palm and covered his hand with hers. She closed her eyes.

"You are a mystery, Kate Beck. Will you skate with me again, soon?"

"Maybe." She opened her eyes.

"Can I give you a good night kiss?"

She nodded and closed her eyes again. His lips brushed over hers lightly and she felt his tongue trace the line in her lips. She opened and his tongue swept over her teeth and touched the roof of her mouth. She put her hand on his cheek and ran her fingers through his hair. He sucked on her tongue and lips and then pulled her into a hug. He nuzzled against her neck and she felt his warm mouth kiss up to her ear. He lightly bit at her ear lobe.

"I have to go in, Jay." She backed up and put her hands against his chest.

"I'll see you tomorrow or later today, I guess. There's a class at eleven o'clock."

She nodded, but didn't answer him. "Good night." She grabbed her box and opened the door.

After she got into her apartment and locked the door, she slid down to the floor. She'd wanted to ask him in, but what did she have to offer? She didn't even own a coffee maker. Her throat started to tighten and she felt tears well in her eyes. This was her life and whether she liked it or not - and right now she didn't like it a whole lot - she'd have to accept this was the way it would be. If she started to tell him about her past and then just up and left, she'd be more broken than she'd ever been. Jay was such a nice man and she didn't think he carried any mean bones in his body.

She set her box with the skates on the floor and brought her knees up under her chin. As much as she'd like to try a relationship, she couldn't do it to him. She'd just have to stay away from the rink and not see him anymore.

Chapter Seven

When Kate didn't show up at the rink the next morning, Jay did some work and then got into his Jeep. It was Sunday and his employees could handle the rink for the day. He drove over to the house where Kate lived and parked along the road. He went up to the front door and rang the bell. An older lady answered and said Kate lived in the basement. Her door was at the back of the house. He went down the driveway, found the door and knocked.

When it opened, he smiled. She wore a pair of gray sweatpants and a navy blue hoodie. Her hair was in a pile on top of her head and she held a book in her hand. As far as he was concerned she looked great.

"Hi," he said.

"Hi."

He stared at her and looked at her beautiful blue eyes. "Do you wear contacts?"

"Ah, no." She stared back at him.

He saw a questioning look form on her face. "Sorry, I just wondered if you'd like to go zip-lining? The park we were at yesterday has a whole bunch of lines and I called. They have a ton of openings today and I didn't have to make a reservation."

"I don't think so. I'm a bit chicken about doing that kind of stuff. I'm not a risk-taker, but thanks."

"How about a movie or something?" He realized he sounded desperate and wanted to kick himself around the block. "Look, I'm sorry. I said I wouldn't be pushy. Let's just pretend I didn't show up at your door." He turned and started up the drive.

"Jay?"

He stopped and turned back. She stood barefoot on the mat outside her door.

"Jay?" she said again.

He saw her look into the apartment and then back at him. There was something in her eyes and he prayed he read it right. He stepped forward and then stopped, but the momentum got the best of him. It took three steps and he held her in his arms with his lips pressed against her warm, full lips. He heard something fall onto the front step and realized she'd dropped her book. She pulled her legs up around his waist and his hand wandered down to her butt. He pushed her back against the door-jamb as their tongues twirled and danced with a primal force. Her warm hands were wrapped around his head and her fingers pulled his hair.

He stepped into the apartment and held her, wrapped around his upper body. She moved her hand and shut the door.

They continued to kiss and then she started to pull his coat off. Jay breathed hard. When his lips separated from hers, all he wanted to do was pull her back and continue the kiss, but she pushed at his coat which slid down his arms. She moved her legs down, stood in front of him and started to unbutton his flannel shirt. He reached down to the hem of her hoodie and pulled it up. She looked up at him and for a second he thought he'd gone too far. She smiled and raised her arms. He pulled it over her head and his penis came to life.

She wore a white, lacy bra and her breasts were gorgeous. She opened his shirt and her fingers traced over his muscular chest. He heard her whisper *Nice* and then her mouth was on his skin. Her tongue snaked around his nipples and she lightly nipped at them. His shaft throbbed against the zipper in his jeans.

He lifted her back up, kissed and sucked on her bottom lip. Her legs wound around his waist again.

He pulled back slightly and half opened his eyes. "Where?" he whispered.

Kate pointed over her shoulder to a short hallway. He carried her into the bedroom and saw her bed. He set her down on the mattress and put his hands on both sides of her face. He leaned over and found her lips waiting for his, and they were warm and passionate. He pushed her down onto the bed and her hands moved the shoulders of his shirt off. With her help he got the shirt completely off and looked down at her.

"You're sure?" he whispered.

"Yeah, you've got protection, right?" She put her hand on his chest.

He smiled. "Yep."

"Good. I'm on the pill, but better to be safe, right?"

"Yes ma'am." His hand moved up her side and felt a ridge running along her ribs. He looked down and saw a mean scar just under the bottom of her rib cage that ran around to her back. "What happened?"

"I was in an accident a long time ago. It's nothing." She moved his hand up and kissed the palm. She then took his thumb into her mouth and spun her tongue around it.

He watched her lips and smiled. "That's very nice," he whispered.

She popped his thumb out and moved his hand to her breast. He cupped the luscious mound in his hand and flicked her nipple through the lace. She pushed up a little and undid the hooks in back. The lace loosened and he moved the straps off her arms. He dropped it on top of his shirt on the floor.

"Beautiful," he said and leaned over. He took the bud into his mouth and his tongue circled it slowly. His teeth lightly nibbled the hard bud and he heard her moan and suck in her breath, quietly. He bit a little hard and felt her squirm underneath him. He kissed down her stomach and when he got to her sweatpants he stood up and started to pull them down. He took them off her legs and then went after the white, lace panties.

He started to lower himself between her legs, but she sat up and put her hands on the top of his pants. She undid the top button and worked the zipper down. His pants started to slide down his legs and she pulled the Jockey underwear down at the same time. She leaned against his leg and said, "Foot up." He put his hands on her shoulders and lifted his foot. She slid them off and then did the same with the other side. He felt her hand move over the scars on his knee and she kissed and licked along his thigh.

She sat back up and looked up at him. She arched her eyebrow and licked her lips. Moving her hands up his legs, she reached around to his rear end and felt his cheeks. He watched as her lips took the head of his shaft and her tongue rubbed the underside hitting a nerve that sent electricity through his system. She kept the head in and slid him into her mouth. Jay closed his eyes and felt the sensation hit his system when she swallowed.

"Kate, your tongue....oh God, that's incredible," he said in a hoarse voice and felt her tongue trace the underside of his shaft again as she pulled back. He put his hands in her hair and held on as she moved a couple more times down his length. She put her hand around his penis and kissed the head again.

She looked up at him. "Where's your condom, Jay?" she asked and stroked him with her warm hand.

He looked down and tried to understand what she'd asked. He finally got it. "Oh right...God your hand, it's...Condom, right, where did my pants go?"

She leaned over and grabbed his jeans. He took his wallet out and found the condom. He dropped the pants and wallet immediately and she snapped the foil wrapper out of his hand and opened the package.

She started to slip it onto his shaft and smoothed it down.

Kate pushed up on the bed and lay back. Jay was in a state of elation. She looked so beautiful and he wanted her head to toe. He crawled onto the bed and stretched out between her legs. His hard penis rubbed against her warm, soft folds and caused her to moan, again. He planted himself on his elbows and kissed her lips.

"Why didn't you come to the rink this morning?" he asked as he pecked at her lips and chin. His hand moved over her breast and pinched her nipple. She squirmed under him and rubbed her warm folds over his shaft.

"I had to do laundry and walk over to the grocery. I have to be honest that you were on my mind a lot during my chores."

"You were thinking about me?"

"Yeah, particularly at the grocery in the beef and laundry detergent sections," she laughed.

"I'm not sure about the soap, but think I get the beef." He kissed her and moved his hand down to his penis. "Would you like to play hide the hotdog?" He pressed the head to her opening.

"I bet I can...find it." She sucked in her breath as he entered her channel. He adjusted his hips and pushed all the way into her. "Oh Jay...you feel so good."

She moved her legs around his waist which caused his penis to slide in another millimeter and he could feel her walls tighten around him.

"Babe, if you keep that up, I'm going to pop too soon." She did it again and he groaned. "Sweet, that is just sweet."

He pulled out and slammed back into her over and over and continued to pick up the pace.

This day just got better and his brain was in such a strange space. He'd never expected anything like this to happen.

"Kate, I'm sorry, but I can't...I'm..." He moaned and pushed into her hard. Her legs tightened around him and her hands grabbed at his back. "Oh Kate, please let this be real."

****

She held him tight and felt his warm breath blow on her ear as she tried to slow her heart rate down. She did think about him most of the morning and when he showed up at her door, it was unexpected. She'd even let herself daydream about him seducing her at the door and wondered if it would happen. She almost felt like she was going to cry. She moved her hand through his hair and let herself believe for a moment.

"Jay, I believe this. I think we're real," she said.

He propped up on his elbow and smiled down at her. "I owe you an orgasm though."

"That doesn't matter. Just don't move for a while. I like this."

"I haven't been with anyone for a long time. I think I got excited too fast."

"That's sweet, but I'm just glad you showed up." She put her hand on his cheek and kissed him. "I kind of daydreamed that you would seduce me at the front door." She crinkled her nose and laughed.

"What time do you get off work tonight?"

"Sunday nights can be pretty slow. I might be able to convince Harry to let me leave by eleven."

"Why don't you come over to the rink, but wear sneakers."

"Sneakers?"

"Yeah, I'll teach you Broom Ball." He wiggled his eyebrows.

"Right, Broom Ball. You wear sneakers to play this game?"

"Uh huh."

"Now you've got me interested." She kissed his lips, again. "I'll be there."

"Cool." He leaned down and nuzzled her neck. "I have something finally to look forward to. I can't wait."

"Me, too. Work will suck."

He started to laugh. "I'm being serious here." He propped back up. "I know I'll be clock watching." He started to move to her side. "I have to get off my knee."

"Oh God, I'm sorry." She moved her leg down so he could roll off of her.

"There's no need to be sorry. I just get stiff." He put his arm around her and she rested her head on his chest. "It hasn't been used much in this position and will need more practice."

She could hear his heart beat and for the first time in a while she felt alive. She didn't know the words to tell him how grateful she felt. He'd pulled her out of the fog she'd existed in for so long. She knew when she had a chance to think, all her doubts and fears would come back to haunt her, but for now she didn't want to think.

She felt Jay tap her on the head. "Hey in there, did I lose you?" he said.

"No, I'm listening to your heart beat." She ran her hand over his chest. "You have a strong heart." She looked up at him. "Sorry, that's kind of weird."

"No it's not." His hand covered hers. "Would you mind very much if I went on an exploration?"

"To the very deepest part of the jungle?" She laughed.

He rolled her onto her back and propped up on his elbow. "Hmm...I didn't think of it that way, but you aren't hiding any bears or tigers?" He lifted the sheet and looked down at their bodies. His lips kissed the tops of her breasts, while his hand moved down to her pelvis and along her hips. He looked up at her and smiled. "You have the most gorgeous eyes I've ever seen, Kate. Whenever you look at me for very long I start to lose myself in them. They're very hypnotic."

Kate felt his finger move down the center of her folds and slide into her channel. She'd been with a man before, a very long time ago, but he'd never done anything like this to her. Jay lightly circled her nub and Kate thought every nerve ending was just lit on fire. She sighed and electricity ran up her legs into her chest.

She opened her eyes and saw his lips move around the nipple on her breast. His tongue and finger made slow revolutions around and around and when he put his finger down hard on her nub and let his teeth graze over her nipple, she was caught up in a storm she'd never felt before. She began to pant and squeaked in delirium. She realized she was experiencing her first ever orgasm. She'd read about them in books, but never felt one capture her body the way this one did. Her back arched as he continued to press on her live nerve endings and then gradually, he slowed the pace down.

His lips moved up to hers and he licked the side of her mouth. She turned her head and accepted his kiss. "Now we're even again," he whispered. "But I'm not keeping score or anything."

They continued to kiss and touch one another for the afternoon. She held on to him and when she realized it was four o'clock and she needed to get ready for work, she reluctantly left his arms and got into the shower. The warm water felt so good and her body felt more alive than it had in years. When she started to wash her hair, the reality of the situation moved into her head and she thought she'd just jumped off a cliff. She didn't want to have the thoughts about leaving Jay and Canon City and tried to shut them off.

****

After Kate got up, Jay lay on the bed for a few minutes. He heard the shower come on and thought about joining her, but felt it might be too soon. They'd only really known each other for a few days, but he'd watched her for a week or two. He didn't want to get in her way.

He swung his legs over the side of the bed and found the spent condom attached to his thigh. He saw a Kleenex box on her nightstand and used a couple of them to pull it off. As he stood up, he glanced into her closet and it struck him as odd. He went over and looked in. There were only a couple of hangers with tops, a jacket and her uniform. She owned a couple pairs of jeans neatly folded on the shelf and on the floor were two pairs of shoes. One pair of sneakers and some snow boots with tread. He saw the box with her skates behind the shoes.

Jay felt himself frown and then got stabbed with a guilt attack. He shouldn't snoop in her things. He walked into the bathroom and tossed the tissues in the garbage can by the toilet.

"Hey, Kate?"

"Yeah?"

"Can I join you?"

"I was just going to get out, but sure, for a minute."

He moved the curtain and stepped into the hot spray. He smiled at her. "You are a beautiful woman."

"Thank you. I haven't showered with anyone since junior high school phys. ed." She started to move so he could get more of the water.

"Have you washed your hair yet?"

"Yes."

"That's too bad. Next time, I get to soap you up. It may have something to do with the laundry detergent aisle." He smiled and pulled her up close to him. "There will be a next time, right?" He leaned over and found her lips open and ready for him.

"If you keep kissing me that way I'll hope for a lot of next times." She moved him back into the water and stepped out of the shower.

He heard her drying her hair and he shut the water off. He opened the curtain and saw she'd already dressed. She set the hair dryer down and turned to him.

"Jay, I only have one towel. I tried not to get it too wet." She picked it up off the toilet and handed it to him.

"Would you dry me off?" He smiled and licked his lips.

"Yes, but..."

"No buts, remember, babe. The only butts are the ones God gave us." He saw her pause.

She continued to hold the towel out and looked down at the floor. "I don't like to be late for work and I need to finish drying my hair."

"Kate, what just happened?" He put his hand around her wrist and tried to pull her toward him. She looked up at him and he could feel fear come off her in waves. He took the towel and let her go.

He watched her turn to the sink with her eyes closed. She clasped her hands in front of her and opened her eyes. As she stared at herself in the mirror, he could only guess at what just happened. She picked up the dryer and aimed it at the back of her head. He slowly dried himself and watched her.

She switched off the dryer and continued to stare at herself in the mirror. "Old fears have a way of creeping back in on me and I start to doubt a lot. It's not you, Jay. It's just me." She looked at him in the reflection of the mirror and leaned against the counter. "I've never had a decent relationship and you seem like a good guy. I want to really try to not let my old fears overwhelm me, but I'm going to need some patience. There are times I freak out really easily."

Jay dried himself off and wrapped the towel around his waist. He stepped out of the shower and moved behind her. They stared at one another in the mirror.

"You've got it, sweetheart." He put his hand on her shoulder. He moved her hair and kissed her neck. His other hand moved around her waist and he felt her hands on his arm. "Kate, I don't know what happened to you and I hope you'll be able to tell me one day. I can feel you shake and I don't like the idea that I scare you. I said it before and I swear it to you again, I'll never hurt you."

"I know. It's not you; please don't think I'm afraid of you. I'm not. I hope I'll get there. I really want to be with you. I'd be stupid to not try."

"Good." He kissed her neck again. "Now, finish drying your hair and I'll drop you at the diner." Jay moved out of the bathroom and got dressed. He used the towel to dry his hair and then hung it over the shower curtain bar.

Kate came out of the bathroom and sat on the end of the bed putting on her socks and shoes. Jay sat down next to her and bumped her shoulder.

"After we have your first Broom Ball lesson, I'd like to show you my house."

"You have a business and a house? How cool is that?" She leaned against his shoulder. "Jay, do you think we're moving a little too fast? We've only known each other for a day or so."

"You know, no one could have predicted our response to one another. When I came over today I had every intention of asking you to go zip-lining. Who knew we were going to have a chemical reaction?"

"The big-bang." Kate smiled.

"I want to kiss you again, my dear. I want to crawl back into bed with you, too. However, you would be late for work and I can't be responsible for making Harry mad at you. He needs to let you off early tonight."

Jay stood up and held his hand out. Kate stood next to him and laced her fingers through his.

"Oh wait, I have to bring some clothes to change into...Oh crap. I completely forgot my laundry."

He smiled as he watched her race off to another door. In a couple of seconds she moved past him with a few more pieces of clothing. He watched as she folded the pieces on her bed.

"I like those lacy under drawers you wear, my dear." He grinned at her.

She looked at him over her shoulder. "I'll have to be sure to wear only the lacy ones when I'm with you."

"This is going to be a really long day," he mumbled as he felt excitement make his shaft twitch.

Chapter Eight

Kate spent the late afternoon and early evening trying to focus on her orders and not Jay. It was very difficult and during her dinner break, she found a quiet corner in the locker room to sit and let her mind wander. She tried to figure out if maybe she'd gone nuts. One minute she'd left to go home and pack up her stuff to leave Canon City. The next minute she remembered the way his arms felt around her and the way his penis twitched in her hands when she'd put on the condom. It caused her to get warm and all the fears returned like a jack-hammer. Both pounded on her - part in her head and the other part below her waist.

She thought about the last eight years and accepted the loneliness she'd felt, but now wondered if there could be more for her with Jay. *Was that the reason she'd let him into her life?* she asked herself. She liked Jay, but was afraid she'd hurt him in the end if she just took off one day. The other question that started to run through her brain was *If she broke it off with him and left now, would it be better for him?*

She didn't want to end it now. She liked him and didn't want to not see him or be with him. All the nights she'd been alone and wanting a man in her life added up to a big zero and it made her brain hurt. She knew her hormones took her over and her logical brain was on ice right now. She decided to take it one day at a time. It was a boring cliché, but that would have to do for now.

When the dinner crowd slowed down in the evening Harry agreed she could leave early. She changed her clothes and left her uniform in the locker.

She crossed the street to the rink and walked through the front doors. She saw Jay sat with his feet crossed on a table. A notebook lay open on his lap and he seemed to make notes. She looked at him and felt warmth run into her body. He was so handsome and giving. All thoughts she'd had of walking away crashed headlong into a brick wall.

She decided then and there, she'd have to figure out a good time and way to tell him the truth about her past. Then she'd know if he could understand and accept her. All of her emotions would be out and she'd know if she should stay or go. She needed to do it soon.

Suddenly, she saw him stare at her. Those gorgeous brown eyes seemed to smile at her and she could feel his arms around her even though he sat in the table area.

"Hey there. Are you coming in?" he asked and put his feet on the floor. He set his notebook down with the pen on top.

"Yes, I am." She smiled back and moved to him.

He stood up and gave her a kiss. "It's been too long since I last saw you."

"Damn, those jobs. They intrude into people's lives way too much." She stood on her toes and gave him a kiss. She set her purse on the table and noticed a roll of duct tape. She picked it up and frowned. "Jay, I've read a ton of romance novels." She looked up at him and still frowned. "You're not into bondage or something?"

"Huh?" He looked at the tape. "Well, what do you know? I hadn't even thought of it, but now that you bring it up." He took the roll from her hand and arched his brow. "Actually, no. This is for something else entirely and I can tell by the look on your face that you're not into bondage either. Which is a great relief, believe me. I'm not into whips and dominating anyone." He held out his hand.

"Thank you for not giving me a heart attack," she said and took her jacket off. "You know that means we're vanilla?" She saw his eyebrows crease in the middle of his forehead. "I've read some of those books."

"I see. If you do have a heart attack I know CPR and would love to give you mouth to mouth." He grinned.

They walked over to the boards and she saw two sawed-off brooms and a red ball.

"Now, first things first." He ripped a piece of tape off the roll and put it on the bottom of one of his shoes. He took off another piece of tape. "Are you a lefty or righty? As in which foot is primary?"

"Right foot." She watched him bend over by her side. The top half of him was behind her and she had a great view of his rear-end.

"Foot up," he said.

She lifted her foot and felt him put the tape on the sole of her shoe. He then grabbed her butt from both sides and bit through her jeans.

"You have a great back side, woman."

Kate started to laugh and patted his cheeks. "Yours isn't too shabby either."

Jay stood up and wrapped his arms around her. "Did you come over here tonight just to feel me up?"

She smiled. "No, I did that this afternoon, but I could be convinced it would be fun to do, again." She placed her warm lips on his and let his tongue into her mouth. She touched her tongue lightly to his and then pulled back. "Sir, you are distracting me from the task at hand. What do I do with tape on my foot?"

He took her hand and she followed him to the entrance to the ice. He handed her a broom and they walked onto the ice.

"This should be easy for you since you know how to skate. Put your right foot forward, you're going to slide on that foot. Push off with your left foot."

Kate did as he said and slid forward. "Who would have known you could slide around on duct tape? Skates will become obsolete."

"Lord, don't say that. I'll lose my business."

Jay showed her how to play the game. Kate felt wobbly at first, but it was fun. They passed the ball back and forth and she thought the practice would help if she came out for the game tomorrow night. She wanted to be there, too.

At one point, Jay passed her the ball and she headed for the markers he'd set up for goal posts. He caught up with her near the boards, wrapped his hands around her waist and pressed her against the rail.

"I believe that is a foul and don't you have to go to the penalty box?" she asked and felt him press his hard penis against her pelvis.

"It's probably an infraction, but we're pretty loose with the rules. It's a foul in basketball and a penalty in hockey." He gave her a quick kiss.

"What is it called in broom ball?" She grinned and liked that she could joke with him.

"Ha, ha, it's the same as hockey, but we don't use the box. These games are for friends to get together and annoy each other. Nothing more."

She squirmed out of his arms and moved the ball to the goal. She turned and smiled at him. "I can think of a couple of ways you could pay me back for that penalty." She batted her eyes at him.

She watched him push off on his foot and come toward her. Kate turned around and moved down the ice. Jay caught up with her, threw his broom down and put his hands around her waist. He held her tight against his chest.

"Tell me all of those ways you want me to pay you back," he whispered in her ear.

Kate laughed and didn't remember any time in her life she'd had so much fun.

****

After midnight, Jay convinced her to come back to his house. She walked in the front door after him. He hit a light switch so they could see where they were going.

"Wow, this is amazing," she said. As she walked into the living room she saw a huge stone fireplace and built-in wooden shelves along one wall. A very long couch sat in front of the fireplace with what looked like a handmade coffee table. In a corner sat a shelf unit with a TV and stereo system. "Did you make this?" She sat on the couch and ran her hand over the smooth wood on the table.

"Yeah. A friend of mine had a cedar tree fall in his yard. I cut a wedge out of it. You can see the knot dead center."

"It's beautiful, Jay. When do you find the time?"

"Oh, here and there. I turn things over to the gang at the rink and work for a couple of days here. The week I did the wood floors upstairs was the worst. It killed my knee and I finally had to hire someone to do the work. Sometimes I don't know when to stop."

Kate stood up and looked around the room. There was a double door off the living room that had what looked like lead plated glass windows. She turned and looked into the dining room The chandelier over the dinner table was some kind of woven material and fit the room perfectly.

"Is there a deck out those doors?" she asked.

"Yep."

"You are incredible, Jay."

He puffed out his chest. "Do you think so?"

She put her hands on his chest. "Yes, I think so. I wouldn't have said it if I didn't feel it."

He put his arms around her waist and lifted her up. He gently put his lips on hers and nibbled her neck and chin. Kate brought her legs up and around his waist.

"You have incredible legs, Kate. They are very strong. Your lips are so warm and your tongue...You're a very good kisser."

"So are you, mister." She ran her fingers through his hair.

"Your mouth really grabbed my attention this afternoon."

Kate realized they were moving and Jay took steps up. They were on their way to the upper floor and she felt her heart start to beat harder in her chest.

"I think I still owe you another orgasm." He turned into the bedroom.

"I thought you weren't keeping score."

"I'm not. I just want to give you the best orgasm in the world, so you'll stay with me for a very long time. And I'm dying to taste you. I only ever did the oral sex thing with one other girlfriend years and years ago. She said it was the best orgasm she'd ever experienced."

Kate almost stopped breathing, and then saw the largest bed she'd ever seen. "Oh my, why the big bed?" she asked and looked around the room.

"See, I'm six-foot-four inches and I've slept in a lot of too short beds over the years. Now I have an extra long, king-sized bed and never have cold feet anymore."

She looked at him. "My bed was too short for you."

"I was so happy. I didn't get the chance to notice." He set her down on the bed, with him between her legs.

Kate started to shake when he knelt down on his good knee. She sat up and put her hands against his chest. "Jay, we need to talk for a second." She saw a question form on his face. He started to say something, but she put her fingers over his lips. "See, I've never done what I think you want to do."

"But you've been with a man before me, right? You took me down into your throat this morning. I mean, you've done that before, right?"

"Yes, we were engaged and, yes, we had sex, but he never did that. I've read about it in books, but..."

"You're telling me he never gave back to you?"

She nodded.

"What a jerk."

Kate could see the wheels turn in his head. "I'm just a bit nervous and a little scared. I'm not sure what to expect."

"Babe, I'm really glad you didn't stay with that creep." He put his hand around her thigh and rested his chin on her knee. "Did he make you take him in your mouth a lot?"

"He liked it, yeah."

"I think I understand why you were so good with me this afternoon. Did he force himself on you?"

"No, I was young and so stupid and felt like I needed to do things like that to keep him happy. It was a long time ago and I want to be here with you. I just thought you should know why I started to shake. You seem to be able to tell when I do that."

"Kate, I was brought up to give and share in a relationship. There's none of this 'give me pleasure to keep me happy' crap. We give to each other and it's fifty-fifty with me."

She put her hand on his cheek. "Where did you come from? Mars?"

Jay started to laugh. "Yes, but I'm not green or gray." He started to unbutton her shirt. "I'm going to do the work tonight. I want you to relax and let me give back some of the pleasure you gave me today. If you start to feel overwhelmed, call me Gimpy and I'll stop."

"Gimpy? I think I can remember that," she said and let him take off her shirt.

"You have the most beautiful bras, but I want it off."

Kate reached behind and unhooked the lacy bra. He slid it down her arms. She leaned forward and pulled his sweatshirt up and off. He moved up and pushed her farther onto the bed. She rested her head back on a pillow and watched him.

Jay lay down next to her and put his warm hand on her stomach. She looked into his eyes and felt warm and safe. She did have a knot in her stomach, but did her best to ignore it.

His lips lightly touched hers and kissed down her chin and neck. His hand cupped her breast as his lips continued to move down to her chest.

Kate felt warmth spread in her stomach and down her legs. An incredible ache started in her channel. She'd had it before, but never knew what to do with it, even with all the books she'd read. He put his lips on her nipple and bit lightly on the hard peak. His hand moved down to her pelvis as he licked and kissed her breast. She felt his fingers undo the top button of her pants and the zipper started to come down. His hand moved into her pants and his fingers maneuvered under the lacy panties she wore. She felt his middle finger move down and touch the button of her desire. He started to move the finger around it lightly and she started to feel an incredible excitement build in her body. She moaned and spread her legs out a little. When his hand came out of the pants, Jay stood up and started to pull her jeans down.

"You still with me, Kate?"

"Yeah," she said and found herself out of breath.

When he got her totally stripped, he got down on his good knee between her legs and pulled one up. He kissed her ankle and bit it a little, which made her laugh.

Kate tried very hard to shut her brain off and just live in the moment. His lips and tongue moved along the inside of her leg and spread them further apart. His warm hands moved up the inside of her thighs and he propped her foot on his shoulder. One of his thumbs tickled over her folds and found her central spot.

"Oh," she sighed and grabbed the quilt under her. The ache in her pelvis flamed up a notch and her back arched as his thumb plunged into her wet core. She closed her eyes as his lips continued to move along her legs and his thumb moved inside her. She released a moan and when his head was in the V between her legs and his tongue teased the nub, she lost her breath completely and grabbed at the headboard. She felt she might be sinking.

His fingers moved into her channel and his mouth covered her nub with his tongue dancing circles around her center spot. Kate felt a tingle flood her pelvis and legs and her back arched again as her breath got caught in her throat. The orgasm flowed over her and she wasn't sure how long she'd sucked in air.

It hit her with all her fears and she felt sad. Now she understood what all the sex scenes in those books she'd read really meant. She felt tears run out of her eyes and when she opened them, she saw Jay propped up over her in a blur. She rolled away from him. Her ears buzzed and if he said anything, she couldn't hear him.

Kate hadn't spilled many tears for over eight years and started to sob with uncontrolled gasps. She didn't want him to see her like this; wrestled out from under his body and got off the bed, with her hand over her mouth. She saw his sweatshirt on the floor, picked it up and made her way to the stairs. She pulled the shirt over her head and the size was so big it hung midway down her thighs. This made her cry harder.

Kate didn't have a clue where she thought she would go. She saw the double doors that led out to the deck and went to it. She figured out the lock and stepped out onto the back porch. Through the flood of tears she saw steps going down to a dark yard. She sat on the top step and put her head on her knees. She wrapped her arms over her head and tried to figure out how to deal with all of this. Jay would want an explanation. Why did it pick now to spill over? Two minutes ago she was in heaven, but it opened something inside her and she'd descended to hell.

She felt Jay's arms wrap around her and pull her into a tight hug. His lips were by her ear and she heard him whisper words to her, but couldn't understand. He ran his fingers through her hair and held her close. When she started to calm down, he handed her some tissues and she realized she could hear what he said. He tried to hush her and apologized for being so aggressive.

Kate sat up and looked at him through a new flood of tears. "No...it's not your fault...don't think that." She took in a deep breath and held it. Slowly she let the air out and leaned against his chest.

After a few more minutes, she said, in a very small voice, "I have to tell you a story." She blew her nose and tried to figure out where to start. She couldn't bring herself to look at him, as the tears continued to roll down her cheeks.

"See, there once was a little girl. When she was six or seven years old, she watched the winter Olympics with her father. She saw the figure skaters and told her parents she wanted to learn how to skate on the ice." She blew her nose again. "So, the parents enrolled her in a class and she practiced really hard because she wanted to be as graceful as the skaters she'd seen. The girl's mother was an over-achiever though and started taking her to skating tournaments. When the girl turned ten, her mother hired a private coach. The coach was really nice and the girl learned a lot, but when she didn't win any majors by the age of fourteen, the mother fired the good coach. She got the girl placed in a training center in Colorado Springs with a coach who turned out to be a tyrant. He yelled at the girl constantly and even hit her now and again."

Kate thought for a minute and wiped her eyes. "Now, for some reason that no one could figure out, the girl could do triple jumps with no problems. For her, those moves were easy and they just came naturally. The new coach didn't want the girl to do triples and made her practice doubles until her toes bled. The girl did fairly well and after she turned sixteen placed well enough in the regional's to skate at the Nationals."

Kate fell silent, again and moved away from Jay's arms. She clutched the tissues in her hand and stared at the dark back yard. She could see everything that happened as though she watched it at a movie theater.

"One night about six months before nationals, the girl met a guy at some party. He was about ten years older than she and paid very special attention to her. He'd watch her skate and then take her to dinner. They went for walks and to the movies. In the first couple of weeks, he took her to bed and she lost her virginity. For a little while, the girl thought she was the luckiest person on the planet. Her mother even approved of the guy and made sure the girl started birth control. It would be bad if the girl got pregnant and all the mother's dreams collapsed. This guy was attractive and very wealthy, and one day her mom said if she played her cards right, she could be set for life. About a month before Nationals the guy asked the girl to marry him when she turned eighteen. It was all going according to plan. The girl felt happy. This was the out she needed to get away from her mother and that wretched coach.

"The night before the short skate at the Nationals, the girl heard her mother talking to the guy. She said not to worry; he'd get paid after the Nationals when the endorsements came in. She said even if the girl didn't win, she'd still place well enough to be able to make deals. She looked cute and had the jumps. Right now, all the guy needed to do was keep the girl happy. After Nationals, if he wanted to break off the engagement, then so be it." Kate stopped the tears and swallowed. "The girl felt hurt and stunned by all that she'd heard. The next morning when she warmed up for the short skate she decided to go against the coach's orders and skate the way she knew she could. In the program, she did the triple axel and a triple-triple toe loop. She landed them perfectly and placed fourth at the end of the day. Her artistry wasn't the greatest, but she could do those jumps.

"In the locker room, after the skate, the coach went nuts. He was furious with the girl and said she'd done nothing more than show off. The girl smarted off and told the coach, she didn't know what he complained about. If she managed to get into the top three his career as a coach would be made. The coach swung at her and hit her in the stomach. He swung at her again and hit her in the chest. She tripped over her skates and landed on a bench. Three of her ribs were broken and one punctured her lung. While she was in the hospital, the tube in her chest that helped her breathe, got infected and created adhesions in the bottom of the lung. She had to have surgery to remove the dead tissue and adhesions and part of her lung was taken out. While she recovered, she found out that the excuse for her withdrawal from Nationals was a twisted ankle. Her mother came in one day and started talking about next year being a good goal. It was an Olympic year, so the girl needed to focus her energies on that, but she would have to start paying attention to what the coach told her to do and not show off anymore. The girl found out that her mother talked to some skating company about her going on tour. The fiancé disappeared and she never saw him again."

Kate looked at Jay and expected to see disappointment or pity on his face. She found he just watched her. The look on his face was sympathetic, but she didn't want sympathy either. "That was eight years ago. When I could get up on my own and the staples were removed from my chest, I walked out of the hospital alone and hit the road. I dyed my hair dark brown and used to put on a lot of make-up. I did everything I could think of to change my appearance.

"At one point, I read about my disappearance. My mother said I'd had a mental collapse due to the pressures I'd been under at Nationals. They were very concerned and offered a reward for any information. My name is Stacy Douglas, but I haven't answered to that name for a long time. I don't know if my mother still looks for me, but if I keep moving, I think I can keep one step ahead of her."

She stood up and moved toward the door. The tears rolled down her cheeks again. "Jay." She looked back at him as he stood. "It's a lot of baggage and I'll understand if you'd rather not be involved with me. I'm not looking for pity. Frankly, I'm not sure what I'm looking for. Thank you for this evening. It was fun and a little mind-blowing." She laughed. "I didn't mean to break down. When I was seventeen and left the hospital, I swore I'd never cry again. I guess there were a few years stored up. I'll need a ride home, if it's okay." It surprised her when Jay stepped up to her and lifted her into his arms.

"Babe, I do feel sympathetic, but really want to beat the shit out of a couple of people. Preferably with my hockey stick. Up until now I've never wanted to hit a woman." He gave her a tight hug.

Kate wasn't sure, but she thought she might continue to cry all night. He acted so sweet and although one of her major fears was being judged, he didn't. He held onto her.

"I think the first thing we need to do is get an attorney and make sure for some crazy reason that bitch you called mother doesn't have any legal hold on you. How old are you, anyway?"

"Twenty-five." She leaned back. "Jay, I can't afford an attorney."

"I have a friend I grew up with and I think he'd be glad to help for a cut rate. In fact, he'll be at the rink for Broom Ball."

"An attorney who plays Broom Ball?"

"Yep, he's great with a broom. I'll arrange to talk to him before the game, all right?"

"Jay, you still want to do that and introduce me to your friends?"

"Of course. This doesn't change anything between us."

Kate got him to let her down. "I'm going back inside. It's cold out here."

They went into the living room and she sat on the couch. Jay grabbed a blanket off an overstuffed chair and put it over her legs. He leaned over and kissed her. "I'll be right back. Someone stole my sweatshirt."

"I can give it back."

"No, I have more. Stay put."

Kate put her feet on the edge of the couch and wrapped her arms around her legs. She heard him move around upstairs. She rested her chin on her knees and closed her eyes.

Something clunked in front of her and she opened her eyes. Jay set two glasses on the table and poured whiskey from a bottle into them. He handed her a glass and sat back.

"Drink this," he said and tapped her glass.

Kate took a sip and felt the warm alcohol run down her throat. "Thank you, that's good."

"Now, please explain to me why I wouldn't want to introduce you to my friends."

She set her feet on the floor and took another sip. "I have a tendency to let people down and..."

"No, stop right there." He set his glass on the table and put hers there, too. He took her hands in his. "It seems to me that a lot of people who should have supported you let you down. I think you know that, too." He turned on the couch and looked straight at her. "I really think your mom should be held accountable, but I'm not sure about the legalities. We'll see what Frank can tell us about all of that tomorrow night. Where was your dad in all this?"

"After my mother and I moved to Colorado Springs, he sort of dropped off the map. I think I only saw him once after we left Portland." She tightened her hold on his hands. "Jay, I need to apologize to you. The other night when we did the skate around I lied to you again." She saw his eyebrows crease and he frowned. "You asked if I'd ever skated in the Nationals and I said no. I just didn't want to go into the whole story and I'm sorry."

He put his hand on her cheek. "That one I can understand and you don't need to be sorry."

She nodded. "What you did to me upstairs was incredible. I've never felt anything so amazing and it was wonderful. I'm really sorry you thought my reaction came from what you did." She started to feel choked up and her eyes filled again. "No one has ever been so kind to me and..." She looked down at their hands. "I think it would be very easy to get addicted to that feeling and you."

Jay leaned his shoulder against the couch. "Do you want to know something funny?"

"Sure."

"Remember I said I knew you?" She nodded. "I saw you skate that short program."

"What? How do you know that you saw it?"

"The other night when we did the skate around, I recognized the making friends with the ice thing. When you said your real name, it clicked completely. Kate Beck just wasn't what I remembered. When the Nationals were on TV, they showed you kneel by the ice and I remember when you gave it a pat. I thought the announcer was going to have a stroke when you did the triples." Jay smiled and sighed. "Now, let's go back to that part where you become addicted to me. I liked that part."

She tilted her head. "I liked that part, too. In fact," she said and moved her hand up his thigh. When her fingers reached his crotch, she felt his penis was still hard. "I think we have a little unfinished business." She bit her lip and looked up at him. "Jay, have you ever made love on your couch?"

He laughed and she opened the button on his jeans. "Let's slide these down." He pushed his hips up and she moved his jeans down. She put her hand around his erect shaft and gave it a couple of light pumps. She moved and straddled his legs and kept her hand on him. "What was it that you said earlier today? I want to play hide the hotdog." She moved her hips and brought his head to her opening. As she let it slide into her channel, she looked into his eyes and heard him groan.

"This is a good way to break in the couch," he said with a low voice.

His hands moved to her hips as she began to move up and down on his hard length. "You feel so good," she said and rotated her hips and tightened her channel around him.

"Oh God," he said, loud. "You did that earlier and it kills me. That feels incredible."

She put her fingers in his hair and kissed his chin and jaw. "I wanted to feel you inside me, just you."

"It's...Oh, God," he moaned and tensed. "Babe, I can't..."

She felt his warmth flood her channel and tightened around him again. He sucked in his breath and put his head back on the couch. His hands gripped her hips and he arched his hips up a little.

"Oh my Lord. Kate, you are incredible," he said between breaths. She started to move off him and he pulled her back down. "Don't move, not yet. I don't want to leave you yet."

She continued to kiss his neck and peck at his lips. He pulled her into a tight hug and then let her move back.

"Are you tired?" His hand touched her cheek.

"A little. I haven't had a good cry for so long. I can't imagine what I must look like." She put her hand over his and kissed his palm. "Thank you for being so patient, Jay. I appreciate that you just listened and didn't ask a lot of questions."

"Just for the record, you look gorgeous, babe and I've been told in the past I'm a good listener. Let's go get ready for bed."

She moved off his lap and hated it when his penis slid out of her. Jay stood up and held out his hand. "Come on."

They walked arm and arm up to his room. In the bathroom, he opened a drawer and pulled out a spare toothbrush. They brushed their teeth together and she hung the brush next to his in the holder. She crawled into the huge bed while Jay slipped off his jeans and sweatshirt. He moved in next to her and propped on an elbow. He shifted the sweatshirt she wore up and looked at the scar on her ribs. He ran his fingers over it and then leaned over to kiss it.

"Kate, I appreciate your honesty with me tonight. Thank you for sharing your story. We've only known each other for a short time, but remember that part about being addicted?"

"Yes."

"I've got it really bad for you, babe. I want to say a certain word, but don't want to scare you."

"Now that you know my dirty past and still want me, it would seem I don't have any reason to be scared of you. You've been patient and so gentle with me. It's more than I deserve."

"You deserve everything and more, Kate. I hope you'll stick with me so I can give you all you could ever wish." He lightly kissed her. "Damn, you're a good kisser," he whispered. "Your lips are killer."

"Thank you."

They talked until four o'clock in the morning. Kate listened to his stories of high school, playing hockey and how much he missed his brother who was in the Army and somewhere over in the Middle East. He said he wouldn't admit that to just anyone. She told him a little about her days in the world of skating and some of the places she'd runaway to in the last several years. She let him ask questions and answered him honestly. They snuggled and kissed and when they fell asleep, Jay wrapped his arms around her body. She rested her head on his chest and felt warm and listened to the beat of his heart.

Chapter Nine

When Kate woke up later that day, she found Jay wrapped around her like a sausage case. His arms held her tight and one of his legs lay over hers. She pushed back against his chest and felt his lips on her shoulder. She smiled and listened to him breathe in her ear. She realized he still slept.

Something made a loud bang in the downstairs area of the house and she thought she heard someone move. She sat up, moved Jay's arms from around her and heard someone come up the stairs.

"Jay, wake up," she said and shook his arm.

"What's wrong, babe?" he asked.

"I think someone is coming up the stairs," she whispered.

"Jason Hager, get your butt out of bed. It's ten o'clock for Pete's sake," a deep voice said and turned into the open door.

Jay sat up. "Oh, shit. I completely forgot."

Kate swallowed and saw a tall man, who looked like Jay, only older, stand in the doorway.

She became aware that she was naked and pulled the comforter up to cover herself.

"Hi Dad," Jay said.

The man's eyes opened wider when he saw Kate and then he smiled Jay's smile. "I think I better go tell your Mom to make breakfast for two." He turned and walked out of the room.

Jay looked at Kate. "How come I feel like a teenager who just got caught doing something bad?"

"I don't know," she whispered, again. "I never experienced that."

He rose and grabbed his pants off the floor. While he put them on, he whispered back to her, "Every other week Mom feels it's necessary to make sure I'm eating right. She brings over casseroles, fried chicken, and other stuff, and then cleans out my refrigerator of spoiled food. I don't always remember to eat everything. I forgot today was the day."

Kate sat on the edge of the bed and slipped her pants on her legs, then stood up and pulled them all the way up. They were the ones with the hole in the knee and she didn't think they looked very nice to meet anyone. She started to put on his sweatshirt and then stopped and took it off. He stopped her.

"Put it on, babe. You look great in that sweatshirt."

"I should go, Jay. This isn't right."

"Kate, I know it's a little early in the relationship to meet my parents, but I guarantee you wouldn't make it out the front door. They're in the kitchen right now and I'm sure Dad's getting asked a ton of questions." He pulled his sweatshirt over his head and smiled at her.

"I don't know. I've never met parents before." Kate felt panic work its way into her brain.

He moved over to her and wrapped his arms around her shoulders. "They're not bad people. Their timing sucks, but for parents, I have no complaints."

Kate put her head on his chest and heard his steady heartbeat. She looked up at him. "What if they don't like me?"

"Sweetheart, I think they're going to adore you. Now, let's brush our teeth, comb our hair and meet the firing squad."

Kate followed him into the bathroom and they brushed their teeth. Jay let her borrow his hairbrush and she pulled her Scrunchy out of her pocket. She knotted her hair into a ponytail.

"Jay, I don't know about this. It seems too soon." She felt herself start to breathe hard and clasped her hands to keep them from shaking. The timing for her did suck. There might still be a chance she'd have to leave Canon City. She knew it would be hard to leave Jay at any point, but he was only one person. The more people she met, the harder it would be and she didn't know if she could take the heartbreak.

"Kate." Jay pulled her into his arms. "I'll be right there with you and I promise they don't bite. I want you to meet them."

"I just don't know. I really should leave." She looked up at him and for a moment felt trapped. She didn't like how this felt one bit.

"You can do this, Kate. You said last night you believe this is real. Believe that I'm not going to let anything hurt you." He put his hands on either side of her face and kissed her. "It's going to be easy."

She put her hand on his arm. "I told you, I disappoint people."

"Not me, never me. You only let me down once when you lied to me, but we weren't dating yet."

"That's not funny, Jay." She frowned and got ticked at him.

"It wasn't meant to be funny, but it's the truth. Are you mad at me?"

"Yeah, a little."

"Good. I'll have to remember that." He kissed her again. "You stopped shaking."

Kate thought about it for a second and he was right. "That's weird."

"Come on, let's get this over with so we can go back to bed."

He took her hand and they started down the stairs. She could hear voices come from the kitchen that went silent when they walked in. The tall man sat at the kitchen table and the woman stood at the stove, frying bacon.

"Good morning, Mom," Jay said and the woman turned around.

Kate saw a very attractive woman with Jay's brown eyes and graying blonde hair. The woman smiled.

"Mom, Dad, this is Kate Beck," Jay said. "We're dating."

"Son, if you've slept with her, of course, you're dating. We're not old-fashioned or dumb." She walked toward Kate with her hand out. "I'm Elizabeth, but everyone calls me Libby." They shook hands. "The tall guy at the table is Mike."

Kate smiled and tried to think of something intelligent to say. "I'm pleased to meet you." Her face heated up and she knew she'd turned red as a beet. She felt embarrassed by his mother's remark about them sleeping together.

"Sweetheart, you don't need to blush. Mike and I are very Twenty-first Century. Why don't you have a seat? Jay, don't just stand there. Pour Kate some coffee." Libby looked at her son and pointed with a pair of tongs. "You do drink coffee, don't you?" she asked and looked directly at Kate.

"Yes."

Jay walked her to the table and when she sat down, he leaned next to her ear. "Mom can be bossy sometimes," he said in a normal voice. "And very outspoken."

"I heard that, young man. Kate, how do you like your eggs cooked?"

"Any way is fine." Kate accepted the cup from Jay and he sat next to her.

"Fried it is." Libby turned back to the stove.

"Where are you from, Kate?" Mike asked.

"Portland, Oregon."

"That's a nice town. We went through there a few years ago. I can't remember what year." Mike smiled.

"It was 2007, sweetheart. We were on a road trip," Libby said over her shoulder.

"That's right. We drove up through Seattle and then came back down along the coast all the way to California. It was in the spring and the weather was great. I think we got lucky."

Kate smiled. If someone told her two weeks ago she'd sit at a kitchen table and have breakfast with someone's mother cooking, she'd laugh in their face. Libby and Mike seemed nice and she could see where Jay got his easy way. The parents drank coffee and told stories while Kate and Jay ate their breakfast. They teased each other and laughed. Kate had never experienced anything so personal in her life. When she was a kid, her family never ate their meals together. It seemed weird.

"Oh, Jay, I heard from Mattie. He's our other son," Libby said and looked at Kate. "He thinks he'll get to be home from the Middle East for Thanksgiving and might not have to ship back out until after the first of the year," Libby said.

"That's great," Jay said. "Matt's my younger brother and he's in the Army." He looked back at his mom. "Is he going to re-up?"

"I think so. He still wants to go to school, but he if he puts in another six years, his school coverage will be better."

"Matt wants to go to school? Wow, the service must have turned him around. He hated school." Jay stood up and got the coffee pot. He refilled the cups around the table.

Kate looked at Jay after he sat back down. "What's 're-up'?"

"Matt initially signed up for six years. When you get to the end of that, he can sign up for another six. He called it re-uping." Jay took a sip of his coffee.

They finished the food and Libby shooed the men out of the kitchen. She'd smiled and told them she wanted a little girl talk. Kate felt instant nerves set in and didn't know what to expect. She got up from the table and helped to clear the plates and cups, then stood by the counter while Libby filled the sink with water.

"How long have you been in Canon City?" Libby asked as she rinsed the plates in the sink.

"About six weeks." Kate watched her load the dishwasher.

"Do you have a job?"

"Yes. I work over at Harry's Diner across the street from the rink."

"I've known Harry for years."

"He's a good boss." Kate's nerves continued and she picked at a hangnail.

"Do you cook at the diner?"

"No, I'm a waitress. I can do simple things in the kitchen - grilled cheese sandwiches, warm up soup and make green salads. If it gets any tougher than that, I get confused."

"Why don't you two come over for dinner sometime this week? You can help me in the kitchen and I can show you some tricks." Libby pulled the drainer up and dried her hands on a towel as the water funneled out.

"I'd like that, but I work nights. Monday and Tuesday are my days off."

"That's workable. Mike gets home by five." Libby turned and closed the dishwasher.

Kate moved back to the table and sat down. Jay's mom acted very kind to her, but she knew from experience not to trust first impressions. Anything could happen. Her nerves jumped up a notch. She could see Jay and his father outside the kitchen window. Jay stared at her and smiled.

"Kate." Libby sat down across from her. "I hope you and Jay can keep things going. He's been at loose ends for a few years and I think you would be good for him. I know it sounds crazy, since we've just met."

"But?"

"No, no buts. There's one thing you should know and I'm sure he hasn't talked about it."

Kate waited patiently and felt like another shoe was about to drop. She couldn't expect everything to work out great.

"The last woman Jay got involved with seemed like a nice girl, but it turned out she'd slept with two other guys. Mandy got pregnant and dragged Jay through a paternity suit. The blood tests proved he wasn't the father, but he became very bitter after that. That happened several years ago and, as I said, he hasn't dated much since. He seems very taken with you."

Kate felt stymied that Libby was so open with the family secrets. She also felt a little embarrassed to know something about Jay that he hadn't told her. "You're right, he hasn't mentioned it, but he hates being lied to." She saw a question form on Libby's face. "The first time Jay asked me out, I lied and said I had to work. Harry came out of the kitchen and talked about my day off. The look on Jay's face..."

"Yeah, that dredged it up. Just be honest with him and you'll be all right." Libby patted her hand.

Kate felt so surprised by the fact that Libby pretty much just gave her blessing to her relationship with Jay. She calmed down for a moment, until the back door flew open and Jay stepped into the kitchen. She jumped in her chair and felt her nerves pop back up.

"Okay, that's enough girl talk."

"I should also mention he's very stubborn sometimes." Libby winked at Kate.

"See Dad, I knew they were talking about me," Jay said to Mike as he came through the door.

"Sorry Lib. I tried to hold him back, but he's gotten stronger than me," Mike said to his wife.

Jay sat down next to Kate and put his arm over her shoulders. She nudged his chest.

"Hi there, babe. I didn't mean to make you jump. Are you okay? Mom didn't torture you too much?"

"I'm fine." She smiled at him.

"Lord, Jay do you think I would torment a perfectly nice young woman, who for some reason, that I'll never understand, finds you acceptable?" Libby asked and winked at Kate, again.

"No, but I know you were probably talking about my evil side."

"Are you still doing blood sacrifices?" She grinned at her son.

Kate wasn't sure where this conversation led to. "We did talk about cooking. Do you like blood stew?" she asked.

Jay, Libby and Mike all stared at her and then started to laugh.

Jay leaned over and kissed her cheek. "Are you teasing me, too?" he whispered in her ear.

Kate didn't answer him. She just smiled and arched her eyebrow.

After Jay's parents left, he threw her over his shoulder and carried her back to bed. They'd only gotten about five hours of sleep and he wanted more before they went to play Broom Ball he told her. They settled into his bed and she tried to sleep for another couple of hours.

For the first few years after Kate ran from her mother, she'd experienced terrible nightmares about things from the past. Even though Jay held her in his arms and she felt safe, she found it hard to rest. Now that her secret escaped out of the bag, she felt nervous that the nightmares might come back. She didn't want to hear her mother scream about her inadequacies or the coach hit her again. She finally did doze off and didn't dream.

Kate heard a buzz and opened her eyes. She rolled over and saw Jay grin at her. "How long have you been awake?" she asked and yawned.

"Not long. I dreamt about you."

"Yeah? I hope it was a good dream." She found his lips waited for her and they kissed passionately for a while and then made love. It lasted long and went slow. Kate orgasmed at the same time as him and it felt more powerful than the night before. She realized that for the first time a man really did make love to her. It wasn't just sex and she knew that the other times with Jay were love, too. It felt like a powerful thought and she almost started to cry, but held it back. She'd done enough crying last night.

When they made it to the shower, it amazed her to find his penis grew hard again. They soaped each other and she stopped. She put a soapy hand around his shaft, looked up at him and smiled. She started to move her hand along his hard length.

"What's going on in the beautiful head of yours?" he asked and brushed his lips over her chin and jaw.

"I know what the word was you were going to say last night, but were afraid you'd scare me."

"Do you feel *it*, too?"

"I do, I think. I've never felt it before and I suppose it could be indigestion." She gave him a gentle squeeze.

"Indigestion? I don't think so woman. Am I going to have to teach you the difference between *it* and an upset stomach?" He pulled her up eye level and put her back against the shower wall. Her legs came up around his waist and he adjusted his rock hard shaft to her opening. He pushed into her and they locked lips.

It wasn't until they got out that she realized they'd sprayed water all over the bathroom. After they dried themselves and the fixtures and mirror, they got dressed. Jay made them a quick, late breakfast of toaster waffles and microwaveable sausages. He said he didn't have time to go through all of his mother's dishes to figure out what she'd brought. While the sausages were in the microwave, he made a phone call and arranged to meet his lawyer friend at the rink around five o'clock. He joked with her about having breakfast twice in one day.

When they arrived at the rink, Frank Donnelly waited for them. He and Jay went to high school together and were friends from kindergarten. He, like Jay, was tall with dark brown hair and dark brown - almost black - eyes. They went up to Jay's office and Kate pretty much told Frank the things she'd told Jay during the night. Frank scribbled in a note book. Kate mentioned one new thing that she hadn't told Jay.

"The last time I saw my mother was about four or five years ago. She said if I didn't come back, she could prove that I'd become a danger to myself and anyone who came near me. She said she'd have me committed to a mental facility where I could rot for the rest of my life."

Jay stood up and faced the wall. He started to pull his fist back like he wanted to punch it, but stopped and put his palm on it flat. He turned back around. "Kate, your mother needs to be shot."

"Jay, I'm going to pretend I didn't hear you say that," Frank said and scribbled more notes in his book. "No more threats against the mother, okay?" Frank looked at him with a stern look. Jay nodded. "Good. Now Kate, from now on you are Kate Beck only. We'll get it legalized down the road, but you have no idea who Stacy Douglas is, if anyone should ask, got it?"

Kate nodded. "That should be easy enough."

"I'm going to need to get some records, so you'll have to stop by my office tomorrow. I'll see to it my secretary has the forms ready for you to sign. You'll have to be Stacy for about five minutes and sign that name. Do you know the name of the hospital you were taken to after the short program at the Nationals?"

"I was flown to Portland. I think it was Portland General, but I'm not too sure of the name."

"Good, it's a start. Do you have any idea if your dad might be of any help?"

"I don't know. I'm not even sure if my parents still live in Portland."

"Okay, I have some work to do. It will probably take a couple of days. It's easier said than done to get records quick, but try not to worry. And you," he pointed at Jay. "Rein in the threats. The last thing I want is to have to defend you, too."

"Yeah, yeah, message received. Can I still kick your butt tonight?"

"You wish. Go tell the gang we're good to go." He stood up and held Kate back. "Now Jay, be a good boy. I want to talk to my client alone for a minute."

Jay looked at Kate. She nodded and he left the room, but didn't close the door.

"This man you were involved with, do you remember his name?" Frank asked.

"David Farnsworth, Jr."

"Very good. We might be able to get him for raping a minor, but it's a stretch. If we threaten him with that, we might get him to help against your mom and all that business about the payoff's. I think our main goal is to get her off your back so you can stop looking over your shoulder. After the game tonight, would you take a minute and write down a list of places and dates where you've had run-ins with her, or her gang of idiots, over the last eight years." He put his hand on her shoulder. "Jay's a good guy and I can see he's stuck on you. Trust him, no matter what. He'll keep you safe."

"I will, thank you. Frank, do you think there is a real chance that I'll be able to stop running?"

"It's too soon to make any promises that I might not be able to keep, but I think we have a very good chance. To try to prove that your mother's badgering you for no good reason, could put us into a grey zone, but let me see what I can find out and we'll go from there, okay?"

"Canon City would be a nice place to stay. I really like this little town, you know?"

"I know. Now are you ready for Broom Ball?"

"I've never played before, but it should be fun."

They walked out of the office and went down the hallway to the stairs.

Kate played the first half of the game and then sat down. Her left lung was on fire and she couldn't keep up the pace. She told Jay to get back on the ice because she wanted to watch his cute butt and daydream about his lips. He wore a worried look on his face and she didn't want him to feel that way. She wanted him to have fun. She felt guilty that she'd brought all of her life issues into his world.

Jay's friend Lark came and sat with her. Lark owned an online company that sold mixes for baked goods and she'd just gotten married last year. Her husband, Charlie, attended veterinary college and she'd become their main support, money-wise for the next couple of years. A lot of the people out on the ice went to school together. Lark and Charlie grew up next door to each other. Before long a couple of other women came and sat. They all got to know Kate and she got to hear all kinds of hilarious stories about Jay as he grew up.

After a while, the men were all with their women on the benches. Stories flew around the rink and Kate didn't think she'd ever laughed so hard. She tried not to think about her mother and what that could possibly mean for her.

"Jay, do you remember Bobbie Reynolds?" Lark asked him.

"Yeah, I remember the dick that always picked on you. I think Charlie beat him up more times than I did in middle school." He put his feet on the bleacher and sat forward. "What have you heard?" He snickered.

"I didn't hear this from Frank..." she started.

"Hey...I didn't say anything I wasn't supposed to. I'm not defending that jerk," Frank said and took a swig of his beer.

"Right. Anyway, he's been charged with drug trafficking. He got caught with a trunk load of something down in Cortez. I heard that if he doesn't name his supplier in Mexico, he could be in prison for a very long time." Lark grinned. "I don't mean to be evil, but he deserves every year he gets."

"What's the name of the guy that used to hang out with him?" Charlie asked.

"Dexter or Jamie?" Jay said.

"Dexter, that's it. He owns a bar up on I-25. It's supposed to be a real skanky place. Every time I drive down from school I pass it. He has it all lit up with neon. Apparently, Dex has stripers male and female." Charlie grinned at his wife.

"As long as you keep passing it, we'll have no issues, sweetie," Lark said and leaned in to kiss him.

Jay laughed. "Maybe we should have a boy's night out there. We could scare the crap out of Dex. You know, haunt him like Scrooge's ghost of Christmas past." He grabbed Kate around the middle, nuzzled her neck and made weird munching noises.

She laughed and Jay moved her legs over his and wrapped his arms around her. "You guys did hear Jamie went from high school into law enforcement?" There were a couple of *what's*, but mostly just shocked expressions. "Yep, he's down in

Texas and is a Ranger. Go figure, right? I saw his mom at the grocery store a while back. I never could understand why he stuck with Reynolds. That guy was the biggest jerk in town for a long time."

"Yeah, he worked hard at making my life miserable as much as he could," Lark said.

Kate saw her look at Charlie and sit up straight.

"But then every time Bobbie harassed me, my prince came along and saved me." Lark put her head on Charlie's shoulder.

"Yeah, and I beat the crap out of him on a couple of occasions." Charlie kissed Lark's nose. "I'd do anything in those days to protect my princess."

"Speaking of, Charlie. I'm still working on the assault charges from the dance last Christmas," Frank said and grinned.

"I'll make an appointment, kind attorney." Charlie put his hands together and bowed in his seat.

It was a fun and relaxed evening and Kate met some new people. Lark invited them to come for dinner soon and Kate said she'd have to check the schedule at work.

They talked until ten o'clock and then the new friends started to filter out of the rink. The security guard, Zack, showed up and Jay turned the place over to him.

They walked hand in hand out to his Jeep and he opened the door for her. After she was in the seat, he leaned in the door and gave her a light kiss. He put his hand on her neck and looked into her eyes.

"Did you have fun?" he asked and kissed her again.

"Yes, I did. I need to start an exercise program so I can keep up out there on the ice. I wish I could have played longer, but I kept losing my breath." She smiled and touched his lips. "I'm really out of shape."

"I think your shape is great and I thought you just wanted to watch my butt?"

"Yes, there was that. I did enjoy watching your behind and your legs and your arms." Her voice faded and she reached around him and patted his rear. "I'll have some questions about the discussions that went on earlier, so I can get up to speed with all of these new people I met tonight."

"Like, what?"

"What was all that business about Charlie being charged with assault at some dance?"

Jay laughed. "Lark's ex-fiancé showed up at the annual Christmas dance last year and got really ugly. The jerk said some pretty nasty things about Lark. Charlie defended her and knocked a couple of the creep's teeth out. I guess the ex is making a stink about it and wants Charlie to pay restitution or some such nonsense."

"I guess it's good that Frank is his attorney," she said and raised her eyebrows.

"He's the best. Do you want to grab anything from your apartment?" He kissed her again and lightly nipped the corner of her mouth.

"Can I sleep in your sweatshirt tonight?" She kissed him back.

"Sure."

"Good, then no, I don't need anything." She smiled at him and saw a crease form between his eyes. "What's wrong?"

"Kate, I'm going out on a limb here, but I want to say this." He put his fingers up into her hair and kissed her one more time. "I'm crazy in love with you. I really loved when I woke up with you this afternoon and I loved the way you handled yourself with Frank. You are an incredible woman."

"Jay, you're going to make me cry, again." She kissed his chin and lips.

"I understand if you're not ready to say the *word*, but I just wanted you to know how I felt."

"I think I can safely say I'm falling in love with you, too. You're so understanding of all my mess."

"Good. Now, I want you to think about moving in with me."

"What?"

"I know it's early in the relationship, but that house needs a woman's touch. It's turning into a man cave. So, just think about it, okay?"

Kate nodded and gave him a hug.

"Let's go home," he said and shut the door. He walked around to the driver's side and got into the seat.

Kate turned in her seat and took off her seatbelt. She leaned toward him and put her hands on either side of his face. She planted a hot kiss on his lips. Her tongue gently pushed into his mouth and traced around his teeth. She sucked on his tongue. When she pulled back, Jay was out of breath and dropped the car keys.

"Wow, what did I do to deserve that?"

She smiled at him and straightened in her seat. "It's been a long time since I've heard the word *home*. It was really nice."

"That's where we're going as soon as I can figure out where the keys went."

Chapter Ten

Kate stayed at Jay's for the next couple of weeks. He'd pick her up after she got off from work and then drop her off the next day before her shift.

The weekend after they meet with Frank, the Mighty Red Rocker's made their mites hockey debut and beat a team from another rink in Canon City. They celebrated at a pizza parlor with some parents and Kate found she enjoyed the company. One of the little boys came up to her and asked if she was Coach Hager's *main squeeze*? Kate laughed so hard it brought tears to her eyes. She teased Jay about it later when they were alone and moved her hand down the front of his pants and cupped his penis. She squeezed him lightly and started to say something about what the kid said, but Jay threw her over his shoulder and they had a very good night.

Early one morning they went back to the Gorge and were going to zip-line, but it was closed. The weather started to change and it turned cloudy. The weatherman said there was a chance of snow. They walked all the way over the pedestrian bridge and followed a path around the rocky hillside. They only spent a few hours walking the paths, as Kate needed to return to town and get ready for work.

When it did start to snow, they headed back to Jay's house and she cooked a meal with help from his mom. Kate held his cell phone between her ear and shoulder and made pizza crust and then added toppings as she was instructed. The pizza turned out pretty good and they ate the whole thing. Then he took her to Harry's Diner.

The snow didn't stick and on her next day off, they drove back into the mountains with a picnic lunch and spent the day hiking. They found a field of wild grasses with huge trees surrounding it like guardians. They saw a large oak tree and spread a blanket on the ground under it. Jay brought along a few pieces of leftover chicken his mother made for him and a loaf of French bread. They ate apples from Washington State and some cheese.

****

Jay leaned back against the tree with his legs stretched out and Kate's head rested nicely on his thigh. They'd been quiet for a while and he realized she'd dozed off.

He thought about the wonderful last few weeks they'd spent together and looked down at her calm and peaceful face. He ran his fingers through her hair and she adjusted a little. Her hand moved around his leg like it was a pillow.

He remembered an occurrence that happened on the last weekend, when his boys were on the ice for practice and smiled. Kate came into the rink and, as usual, got her coffee and went to sit on the bleachers. It was hard for him to keep his eyes off her and at one point, he'd turned practice over to an assistant.

Jay caught her eye and crooked one of his fingers, beckoning for her to follow. They'd gone down a hallway to the empty game room.

"What's the matter, Jay? Is there a problem?" she'd asked.

He looked down at her with a most serious expression and took her coffee cup out of her hand. She'd exclaimed when he'd picked her up and pressed her back against a wall. He kissed her hard and then nuzzled her neck.

"Babe, you are so tempting. I just want to feel you up for a minute." He continued to run hot kisses up her neck to the base of her ear.

"Maybe I should leave. I don't want to divert your attention away from the boys." She giggled and brought her legs up around his waist.

"When you're not around, I'm still diverted. We've got to figure out a day to just stay in bed and not get up. God, I want you so bad right now." He moved his hand up under her shirt and fingered her breast through the lace on her bra.

She'd moved her hands around his neck and pushed her pelvis closer to his. She'd rubbed her hot jeans over him and they locked lips. Their tongues touched and a gentle kiss turned into a storm.

"Ah, Mr. Hager?"

Jay heard a voice from far away. His head popped up and he looked toward the doorway. Nine-year-old Jeff Mather stood and looked at them. He held onto his hockey stick and wasn't wearing his blade guards.

"Mr. Hager, we were wondering if we could have a fake game today?" Jeff asked.

Jay looked down at Kate. The look on that young boys face almost made him crack up laughing, but he'd known he needed to be serious. It turned out all right and the boy didn't seem to notice Kate at all - or so Jay thought.

He smiled at the memory and continued to move his hand through her hair. He hoped that Frank could get her situation under control and she would always look as peaceful as she did now. He'd spend a lifetime under trees on picnics if it would help Kate to find some peace.

He thought again about the day at the rink and looked out at the trees and grasses. He chuckled at the memory. He felt Kate move a little and her hand continued up his thigh. He saw her eyes flutter open.

"What's so funny, Jay?" she asked and closed her eyes, again.

"Oh, I was just thinking about the other day when we were caught in our little indiscretion in the game room," he said and lightly touched her ear.

"Yeah, it's a good thing your hand under my shirt wasn't in full view of the doorway."

"Jeff's dad, Rick Mather, came up to me later. He said Jeff told him he'd caught us kissing the way he sometimes does with Jeff's mom. Jeff told him it was gross." Jay laughed again and then moved her hand and slid down on the blanket next to her.

She opened her eyes and he saw a smile creep onto her lips. "I guess you'll need to be a little more careful when you decide to feel me up."

Jay's hand was already under her shirt and moved up to tweak her nipple. "I just hope Jeff finds out one day that kissing isn't gross." He pressed her to her back and brushed her lips with his. When she sighed, Jay's penis became harder than it already was and pushed against his jeans. His hand moved down her side and he lifted his pelvis off her to undo the button on her pants.

"Jay, really? Here? What if someone else is out hiking today?" She gasped around his kiss.

He looked up and around the field. He then smiled down at her and moved her zipper down. "Yeah, here. There's nobody around and if we don't I'm going to be really uncomfortable on the hike down to the parking lot."

He helped her get her pants off and when she mentioned it was a little chilly, he wiggled his eyebrows and smiled evilly. "Let me warm you up, Miss Beck."

They made love twice out in the field that day and his legs wobbled on the way back to his Jeep. These were incredible days.

Chapter Eleven

Edna Hardy looked out the window from the second floor suite at the Holiday Inn. The sky was beautiful to look at, but her view of the parking lot stunk. *So much for calling this a suite,* she thought. Canon City wasn't Denver and, as far as she was concerned, no quality hotel existed in this town. She turned and looked around the room.

"Yeah, right. This is a suite," she said and shook her head.

A buzz came from her cell phone. She walked over to the table and picked it up. "Tell me something I won't find disappointing, Ken."

"We found her. Brad's inside the skating rink and will let me know if she moves. I'm about two minutes from you. I'll be in the front driveway when you come down."

Edna smiled. "Very good, I'll be there in a moment." She clicked off the phone and grabbed her purse.

She made her way down the one flight of stairs and waited for her assistant to pull up to the front of the hotel. This day turned out better that she thought it would. When the giant black SUV pulled into the drive, Edna got in and buckled the seat belt.

"What is the plan?" She glanced at Ken and saw him shrug. "Perhaps, when she leaves the rink we could knock her out and take her," she said.

"Mrs. Hardy, that would be a great idea if it wasn't against the law and a federal offense."

"Ken, you have no sense of adventure or balls. Let's go over to the hovel she lives in and wait. I think I know how to get her home sooner than later." She took her cell phone out of her purse and flipped through some numbers. She found the one she wanted and hit send. After a couple of rings a woman's voice answered. "Hello Monica. This is Edna Hardy. My daughter is at the skating rink and we need to figure out a way to get her out of there. Can you think of anything?"

"Yeah, I see her and I think I know of a way to get her on her feet."

Edna put the cell phone down. "Ken, is Bradley wearing his black leather jacket this evening?" He nodded. She brought the phone back up. "Dear, look for a tall bleach-blonde man wearing a black leather jacket. His name is Bradley and he can help you."

"I see him," Monica answered back.

The line went dead and Edna looked at the phone. "She hung up on me. How very rude." She shook her head and snapped the phone closed. "The courtesy in these small towns is atrocious or doesn't exist. Call Brad and tell him to work out something with that woman."

****

The next Red Rocker's game was that Saturday night. A team from Pueblo came into town to play against Jay's team. Kate traded shifts with another waitress and walked into the rink with Jay. He gave her a kiss and told her to cheer hard.

She got a cup of coffee and made her way to the bleachers. She sat with some of the parents and they watched the kids warm up on the ice. Lark and Charlie Stone came in and sat with her. Everyone seemed to be in a good mood and the common thought was that the Rocker's could beat the visitors easily.

Kate looked over at Jay and saw he and the assistant coaches go over plays for the game. She smiled and felt warmth spread through her veins. She thought for a minute how wonderful it was to watch him. Jay took great care with the kids and seemed to relate to them on their level.

As she admired him from afar, someone sat down next to her and when she looked, found it was that woman, Monica, who'd tried to seduce Jay. Lark and some other people around the rink told her the woman caused trouble and was a pain in the butt. Jay said that, too. Kate wished she'd sat somewhere else.

"Hi, we haven't met. I'm Shelby's mom; you've probably seen her skate. I've noticed you sitting here on Saturday mornings," Monica said and tossed her dark red hair over her shoulder. "I'm surprised you're still here."

"Why would you be surprised?" Kate asked and felt a knot form in her stomach.

"Jay told me you were on the run from your mom. I just figured you didn't stay in one place for very long."

Kate stared at the woman and wasn't sure she'd heard her right. Jay told her that Monica lied through her teeth, but how else would she have known about her mom. "What?"

"Sure, he fucked me up in his office last week while you worked your pathetic job over at the diner. He told me everything. You do know he called your mom? He wants the reward money."

Kate felt a sharp pain stab at her heart. She looked across the ice and saw Jay. He looked back at her with a very deep frown. He turned to one of the other coaches, said something and then started across the ice. She knew he headed her way. Kate started to stand up, but Monica grabbed her wrist and pulled her back down.

"See that guy over there, the one in the black jacket with the blond hair by the benches? He's here to take you back to your mommy. You know, Jay laughed and said your story sounded so pathetic he just had to play with you."

Kate pulled her wrist out of the woman's hold. "Keep your fucking hands off me," she hissed. She stood up and moved down the bleachers to the floor. She saw Jay come toward her, and bolted for the front door. She got to the parking lot and moved through the cars. She knew Jay trailed behind her, but if he said anything, she couldn't hear it. There was nothing but a buzz in her ears. That woman's voice kept whispering over and over that he'd called her mother and it wouldn't shut up. Panic overtook her and all she could think was she needed to get out of Canon City now.

She felt a hand wrap around her waist and pull her off her feet. She tried to fight him, but Jay's arms were too strong. She heard him say to calm down and tell him what that bitch said to her.

Kate took a breath and said very calmly. "Let me go."

"Kate..."

"Just, please, let me go," she growled and felt his arm loosen. She moved away from him and found it hard to catch her breath. Her chest hurt and burned as she tried to take in air. She started to walk toward the street, and felt Jay right behind her. She could feel him watching her and it stung the back of her neck. She stopped and looked at him. Her eyes began to sting, but she would be damned if she let herself cry. "Why did you tell Monica? Of all the people in Canon City, why her?"

Jay frowned. "Tell her what?"

"About me, asshole. She knows about my mother. Monica told me that you've contacted my mother to let her know I'm here in Canon City. She said you wanted the reward. There's only one other person who knows about me and I doubt Frank would break client privilege, unless you two have worked it out. I suppose the reward would be worth it."

He moved toward her, but Kate backed up a step. "Babe, I told Monica nothing. I'd never do that. She's a liar and you've got to trust me."

"Trust you? God, I fell for it so easily. You give me that story about hating to be lied to, but you were the one who lied. I fell for everything you said."

Kate's brain jumped all over the place and she only knew one thing for certain. She had to leave. She'd never be able to breathe freely if she stayed. Frank didn't have the first clue what he was up against. She saw the guy in the black jacket come out the front door of the rink. She turned toward the road.

"I don't know who or what to trust or believe. I only know one thing and that is I've got to leave, now. There's someone here and I can't go back to that life, ever."

She sped up her pace, but Jay kept up with her. They passed the diner and she heard Jay on the phone with someone. He snapped the phone closed.

"Frank will meet us at your apartment. We need to know what to do."

She stopped and turned to him. "No, *we* don't. I'm leaving. I must have been crazy to think I could have some kind of normal life. My mom used to say I wanted too much and I guess she was right. I thought you were an exceptional man, but, boy was I blind. So go back to the rink, Jay. Your little whore is there, waiting. We're finished."

Jay grabbed her arms and looked at her. "What else did she say to you? Besides the crap about me calling your mom."

Kate looked up at him and felt so torn. His face and eyes didn't look like he lied and then his nostrils flared. She wanted to believe him, but all of her trust issues surfaced. She pushed away from him, but he tightened his grip on her arms. "It doesn't matter, Jay. Just stay away from me."

"It matters, Kate. Tell me what she said."

She looked away from him and tried to get out of his hold. "She said you fucked her in your office and told her everything. She said you laughed and that my story was pathetic."

"And you believed her?"

"I have no clue what to believe. I don't know you well enough..."

"You know me, Kate."

She pushed away from him and started back to her apartment. "Go back to the rink, Jay. There's nothing more to talk about. I have to get out of here." She turned down the driveway to her apartment and saw a black Ford Bronco parked with the engine off. She stopped dead in her tracks. Another hand wrapped around her left arm and she knew it wasn't Jay since he stood on her right.

When she saw the man in the black coat, she tried to get out of his grip, but he pulled her toward the Bronco. Kate squatted down and the man continued to drag her. Jay stepped in front of her feet and grabbed a handful of the man's jacket. He swung up at the guy and she could hear a bone crack. The guy landed on his butt and held his face. Blood ran between his fingers and he moaned. Jay leaned over and helped her get up.

She heard a door open on the Bronco and saw a platinum blonde woman step out onto the driveway. Kate backed up a step, but didn't know where to run to that would be safe from the woman who grinned at her. All she needed to do was get into her apartment, get her things packed and go to the bus station.

"Hello Stacy, long time, no see," the woman said. She reminded Kate of a snake. "Are you ready to come home?"

Kate pulled her arm out of Jay's hand and looked at the woman who'd given birth to her and thought she might throw up. She heard a car pull up along the curb on the street and glanced back. She saw Frank get out of a BMW. He walked up and stood next to Kate. She saw him glance down at the guy with the bloody nose who still lay on the ground.

"Mrs. Hardy, your daughter doesn't want to speak to you right now," Frank said. He took a small wallet out of his jacket pocket and pulled out a business card. He handed the card to the woman. "You can call my office to set up an appointment. She won't talk to you without me present." He turned back to Kate and Jay and motioned them to the house. "Let's go inside. It's cold out here."

"Stacy, please, there is so much you need to know. There've been so many changes. Just talk to me," her mother said and tried to move toward her.

"Mrs. Hardy, there's nothing she wants to hear from you right now. Get back in your vehicle and get out of here. There will be a time and place to conduct a conversation." Frank looked at Kate and pointed to her doorway.

Kate walked to the side of the house with Jay and Frank following. She took her key out of her pocket and opened the door. As she walked in, she moved away from Jay and went to the other side of the living room. Her heart raced and pounded in her ears. All she wanted to do was pack her bag and get out of here. She didn't want a conversation with her mother and she didn't want to talk to Jay or Frank.

She couldn't look at either man. She didn't know if what Jay said was true or not. She didn't know who she could trust. Her body felt numb and she just wanted to catch the next bus out of town.

"I was going to talk to you two after the game. How about we all sit down for a minute?" Frank said.

"I'm too wound up and just fine standing." Kate leaned against the wall and crossed her arms over her chest. There wasn't much time. The sooner she left Canon City and changed her name again, the better.

"Okay, your mother at one time controlled your management as a skater, as I'm sure you're aware." Kate nodded. "That all ended seven years ago when you turned eighteen. The contract expired. So as far as the skating is concerned, she has no cards to play one way or another."

She saw Frank look at the kitchen. He went in, grabbed a straight back chair, carried it into the living-room and sat down.

"I found out something interesting. Your mom has some writer on hold to do a biography of you. She seems to think she can make millions on your story, which makes no sense. You're a wonderful person, Kate, but rarely do bio's sell that well." He rested his elbows on his knees and tented his fingers. "Kate, I want you to hear what I'm going to say. Are you with me?"

Kate saw Frank look at her with a very angry stare. "Yes."

"You're sure?"

"Yes, Frank, I can hear what you're saying," she said and felt her own anger begin to build.

"Your mother no longer controls your life. She has no control unless you let her. The idle threats she made about committing you to a mental hospital are nothing. If she continues to badger you, I've prepared a harassment law suit and she'll be slapped with a restraining order. Do you understand what I'm telling you, Kate?"

"I think you're saying that I let her push me around all of these years when I could have just told her to fuck off and leave me alone."

Frank chuckled. "You got it, but I think she trained you pretty well to fall in line. Now, I want you to think about one thing only, if you run again she wins. I'm pretty sure you don't want that."

Kate opened her mouth to say something, but didn't know what she wanted to say. "I understand," she said and looked down at her hands. "Why did you call her Mrs. Hardy?"

"She's remarried. I don't know the details yet, and we still have some things to check out. It looks as though your parents divorced at some point. I've tried to reach your father, but haven't found him yet.

Look sweetie, I don't want her to bug you anymore. I know you've been staying at Jay's, but she'll probably be able to figure that out and find his house. This might be an ideal time to borrow your good friend's cabin."

She frowned at him. "Who's my good friend?"

"Frank thinks he's being funny. It's his cabin," Jay said.

"The words *thank you* are not in Jay's vocabulary, Kate. You're going to have your hands full with him; you should know that up front. Your mom can easily find out where Jay lives. I think you two should go to the cabin and enjoy a nice relaxed week or two off. I'll let Harry know you're away on an emergency, but should be back soon."

"No, I have to work and I'm not at Jay's anymore. We're finished." She crossed her arms and looked at the floor.

"I'm not sure what's happened here..." Frank said.

She looked up and saw Frank look back and forth between her and Jay. "I don't think..." she started but Jay interrupted her.

"Frank, could you come back to lawyer mode for a minute?" Jay asked. "I need for you to defend me."

Kate saw Frank arch his brow and look, again, from Jay to her and back. "Okay, what have you done?"

"Tell him what Monica Everett said to you at the rink." Jay crossed his arms and looked at her.

"Oh, God, not the forked tongued bitch?" Frank groaned. "What did she do?"

Kate swallowed and froze. She felt embarrassed and realized she'd let Monica play her. The look on Jay's face killed her and she knew she'd hurt him by believing the woman. It didn't matter, though. She'd only hurt Jay in the long-run and it was best for him not to be involved.

"She told Kate that I contacted her mother. Monica also said I fucked her in my office at the rink," Jay said.

Frank stood up and walked over to Kate. He took her hand in his and looked her in the eyes. "Sweetheart, I'm only going to tell you this once and if you ever fall for her lies again, I will spank you myself. Monica Everett is a pathological liar. I don't know if I've ever heard her tell the truth and I've known her since kindergarten. Ignore the words that come out of her mouth, Kate. It wouldn't surprise me if she was the one who called Mommy Dearest, but how did she know about it?"

"I have no idea, but I intend to find out," Jay said.

Kate looked at Jay, again and saw him shrug his shoulders. He looked pissed and she didn't think he would ever forgive her for the way she'd treated him. It would have to be. She'd just have to understand if he wanted nothing more to do with her.

"As for the other thing she said, she's been after a couple of men in town since high school and we all hold her at an arms distance. There's no way Jay would screw her anytime, anywhere. To save your sanity, Kate, just disregard her and don't let her push your buttons again." Frank looked at them both. "It would seem you two need to talk. I'll be in touch. I'm going to make sure the Bronco is gone. If I come back inside it's because she's still out there and we'll need to call the sheriff."

Kate didn't even realize Frank left the apartment. She stared at Jay. The look on his face killed her and the realization that she'd blundered by believing Monica made her very angry at herself. She said terrible things to him and didn't know what to do.

"I'm really sorry. I never meant... Maybe someday I'll be able to not freak out...I mean I don't know how..." She looked up at him and wanted to hold him, but thought she might have gone over the line and hurt him so badly he wouldn't want to be with her anymore. "I'm so confused and have a lot to learn," she said quietly and looked down at her hands.

She saw his sneakers down by her feet and felt his fingers under her chin. He moved her head up. His brown eyes were pinched and looked very intense. He pulled her into a hug. She put her head on his chest and wrapped her arms around his waist.

"When I saw Monica talking to you, I freaked out. I could tell by the look on your face it wasn't good." He put his hands on her shoulders and moved her back. He looked directly at her and Kate started to worry this was the end. "Babe, this is lesson number one and it's something you need to take very seriously. The way it is with me, and those around me, family and close friends, is that we take care of things that are important to us. My mom is already over the moon about you and plans to take you shopping even though she's only known you for an hour. I'm giving you early warning. My parents instinctively can tell when something or someone is important to their sons. Honey, I adore you and us and everything that means. This may sound crazy, but we fit together in a really weird way. So, part of being involved with me is putting up with my over-protectiveness. I...well..." he smiled. "I won't say that *L* word because I don't want to scare you, but since I do, you've now got a family and friends that care for you." He stood up straight and put his hand on her cheek. "I know you have trust issues and it will take some time for you to rely and have complete faith in me. I can live with that. I need for you to understand that when I'm involved with someone who makes me catch my breath when they walk in a room and how you can move so gracefully on the ice and waiting tables, I'm involved for good. You're the only one I want by my side, Kate, my beautiful woman. That's enough of lesson number one."

Kate started to open her mouth, but her voice caught and a tear rolled down her cheek. She put her hand over his and closed her eyes. She didn't want to sob. "Jay," she whispered and her lips trembled. "Thank you. I was so afraid I'd screwed up completely and...and..." She shook her head and tried to get a complete thought together in her brain. "My mother can be very mean and I really have no right to ask you to put up with..." She stopped when he put his fingers over her lips.

Jay pulled her back into his arms and held her tight. He wrapped his arm around her head and kissed her hair. "I can deal with her. You don't need to worry about that. Okay? There's no need to think that you screwed up. Just know that we're together and I'd never in a million years do anything to wreck what we've got, okay?" He moved her back and wiped the tears off her cheeks.

"Okay," she said and tried to smile. "Oh Lord, the game. You should go back to the rink. The game's probably still going on and the kids need you."

He put his hand on her neck and looked down into her eyes. "It's only a game, Kate. It's not as important as you are."

She looked up at him. "I'm not that selfish and I want to go back. If Monica is still there, I want to see her face when we walk in hand in hand and you give me a hard kiss with lots of tongue."

"Oh baby, I like where your head is at. Maybe you want to go check your face. Your make-up got a little smeared."

Kate went into her bathroom and looked in the mirror. "A little smeared is being kind, Jay," she said and grabbed a Kleenex to wipe the mascara off her cheeks.

On their way back to the rink they discussed going to Frank's cabin, but decided it would just be another win for her mother. Kate would stay at his house for now and they would try to continue to live.

Jay went back to coach the kids and Kate found that Lark saved her seat on the bleachers. She sat down and wished she'd gotten a cup of coffee. She saw Monica sat a few rows from her. They glared at each other.

"So, what happened? Where'd you head off to?" Lark asked and leaned on her shoulder.

Kate looked at the pretty brown haired woman and found Lark's husband looking at her, too. Kate smiled. "It was a mis-understanding. It's all right now."

"I saw that witch talk to you. Was it her fault?" Lark asked and glared down at Monica.

Kate noticed that Lark's voice had gotten louder and tried to keep her quiet. "She said some nasty things about Jay and I was stupid enough to buy it. I've definitely learned a lesson this evening."

"Sweetie, don't believe a word that comes out of that dragon woman's mouth. She's nothing but lies," Lark said, loudly.

Kate saw Monica turn around and glare back at Lark.

Charlie reached over to his wife. "Lark, that's enough. I think you've gotten the point across," he said and planted his lips on hers.

Lark turned back to Kate. "I love my husband very much, but he is the pacifist in our family."

She was introduced to some other new people that sat around them. One of the men, Eddie Sykes, was a nurse at the community walk-in health clinic. He and Lark talked about the new women's center that would be opening in a week. They were both very excited about it. Eddie said they would have an outstanding doctor come in and start to help out in the next couple of weeks. They were also going to have three full-time clinical psychologists who would start to schedule right away. Kate wondered briefly if Jay might have had something to do with this introduction, but then realized her trust issues were starting to rear up and shut them off. *Maybe I should make an appointment with one of the head doctors,* she thought. For now, she needed to trust in Jay and that was the only thing that mattered.

During the break between periods, Jay moved away from the team and walked directly to Monica. He motioned for her to follow him and she did. He came back after about five minutes, found Kate and stepped up to the bleachers where she sat. He leaned over her and said into her ear, "Monica has been banned from the rink. I told her Shelby's coach would meet them in the driveway or her grandmother could bring her, if the kid is going to continue with lessons, but if Monica steps through the doors, she'll be asked to leave by security or the staff. She called your mother."

"Did she say how she found out about my story?" Kate asked.

"Apparently, the night we came here for the Broom Ball game and met with Frank, she stood outside my office door. When Frank asked me to leave so he could talk to you, she heard the conversation and did a little research of her own. She figured out who you used to be and we know the rest."

Kate looked up at him and almost started to cry. "Thank you, sweetheart."

He gave her a kiss and then went back to the team. The Mighty Rocker's won that night three to one.

Chapter Twelve

Later that evening, Jay rolled over in bed and realized Kate wasn't there. He sat up and saw she stood by the window. The light that came in through the glass gave her a ghostly glow. She looked beautiful.

"Hey, babe. Are you okay?"

She looked over her shoulder at him and smiled. "It's snowing."

Jay got up and walked over to her. He put his arms around her waist. "Damn, look at that and it's only October. It's early this year," he said and looked out the window. The trees and ground in the back of his house were dusted white. "I guess the picnic a week ago might have been the last for the season. This probably won't hang around long even though it's gotten colder."

"It looks so peaceful." She leaned against his chest. "Jay, babe." She laughed. "I need to use endearments more."

"Why are you shaking?" He kissed the top of her head.

Kate moved his arms from her waist to around her shoulders and kissed his arm. "I hate to admit this, but I'm scared silly." She entwined her fingers with his and continued to kiss his arm.

"You have every right to be scared, but you're safe here with me. Your mom looked like a blonde wicked witch."

"As I said earlier, she can be really mean when she doesn't get her way. Once when I was little, my dad told her *no* about some car that she wanted. I can't even remember what type it was, but she got it within a week. My dad stayed angry with her for a long time and it changed the way he'd treated me." She turned and wrapped her arms around him. "I wish I'd known him better."

Jay kissed her forehead. "Come back to bed. It's cold in there and I missed you." He steered her to the bed and sat her down. "That reminds me, wait here one second." He ran down the stairs and found his coat. In the pocket was a small flat box. He pulled it out and ran back up the stairs. When he got back to the room he found Kate hadn't moved from where she sat.

He sat next to her and turned on the lamp that stood on the nightstand. "First of all, I want you to know this nightstand is yours. I emptied out the drawers so you can put whatever you want in there." He saw a surprised look on her face. "Secondly, all the drawers in the right hand side of the bureau are yours, too. They're all cleaned out and ready for your girly things. The top drawer in the bathroom is also ready for your make-up and stuff."

"Oh my God, when did you have the time?" she said.

"When you were at work last night and, I also bought you this." He put the box into her hands.

"What is it?" She looked at it and then back up at him.

"Open it." He waited until the box was open. "It's a cell phone. I've programmed my number and Frank's into it. You can call me whenever you want to...oh, and if you want me to change the ringtone, I will." He picked his phone up from the nightstand and hit a button. In a couple of seconds the lights came on her phone and a voice said, "You're mine, babe."

"Is that you?"

"Yep. Every time I call, you'll know it's me. When the regular ring goes off it will be somebody else. The other great thing is the GPS in it. No matter where you are, I'll be able to find you, but please, leave the phone on. If it's turned off, I won't be able to locate where you're hiding."

"Jay, this is incredible. Thank you. It's my first cell phone ever. You'll need to teach me how to use it. I don't know what to say."

"This thing," he said and pointed into the box. "It's the charger. We'll have to find a place to plug it in. In the meantime, come back to bed and keep me warm."

She set the phone back in the box and they crawled into bed. He wrapped her in his arms and she rested her head on his chest.

"Kate, I really wish you'd take Frank's offer and not work for a couple of weeks. He can explain it to Harry and you won't lose the job." Jay felt concerned for her safety now. The way that jerk held her arm and tried to drag her to the Bronco this evening made him think they wanted to kidnap her.

"There will be other people around the diner and I'll give Harry a heads up if anything bad starts to happen. It's just another situation where if I hide, my mother wins."

"I know. I'd feel better if you came to the rink with me and hung out there."

She put her chin on his chest and looked up at him. "Jay, if I did that, once the skating classes finished, I'd be bored out of my mind and in your way. You wouldn't get any work done, because I wouldn't want to keep my hands off you." She propped up on her elbow and kissed his chest. "You will drop me off and pick me up. In between that time, I'll wait tables, refill salt and pepper shakers, bus tables if needed and all the usual waitress activities. I promise not to leave the restaurant without you."

"I suppose I could hang out there," he said.

"You'd be bored."

"Then just promise me one thing." She nodded. "If something doesn't feel right and you think you're going to panic, call me immediately. I'll be across the street in two seconds. Okay?"

Kate scooted up and kissed his lips. "You know, you've made it very hard for me not to fall in love with you?"

"That's my plan, babe. I'm going to keep you with me and we'll grow old together." He felt her lips lightly touch his and her teeth grazed his chin. "Sweetheart, if you keep this up, I can't be responsible for my actions." He rolled her onto her back and nuzzled her neck.

"That's my plan, babe," she whispered.

Chapter Thirteen

Jay dropped Kate at the diner. He leaned over, kissed her and then whispered that he'd rather go back home. She still felt very scared about her present situation, but wanted to work. She needed the tips to add to the stash of money she saved for occasions like these. She didn't know if she would be able to not run with her mother lurking around Canon City.

Her new cell-phone sat in her pocket and was turned on. She went in, and after she put her purse into her locker, she found Harry and explained to him about the situation. He acted very supportive and said if he could help in any way, to just let him know. He patted her hand and said not to worry, he'd watch her back.

The customers were pleasant for a Sunday night and, although it wasn't busy, a steady stream came through the front door. Kate got into the flow and kept a smile on her face. After a couple of hours, the pace slowed down. Harry let Shar leave early after Kate said she could handle the rest of the night.

Jay showed her how to use the cell phone, but she still felt sketchy on taking pictures and writing notes. All she really wanted it for was to make calls and at this point he was the only one she wanted to call.

An older couple came in and she seated them. They'd been to some movie over in Pueblo and were starved since they didn't have popcorn. She gave them a menu, but they told her they didn't need to look at it. They knew exactly what they wanted. She started to take their order, when she heard a male voice say "You're mine, babe." She looked at the man and woman and started to laugh.

"Excuse me a moment," she said and moved to the back hallway.

"Why are you laughing, sweetheart?" she heard Jay ask.

"Can you tell me how to turn the ringtone down or make the phone vibrate? I just waited on an elderly couple when it went off and I got a very strange look from them."

Jay laughed on the other end. "I'm not sure. I'll have to look at it later. Call me back when you're alone."

"Okay." She went into the restaurant and back to the table she waited on. "Sorry about that, folks. Where were we?"

She got the order and put the ticket on the wheel. She heard the bell over the door ring and turned, ready to walk to the end of the counter and seat another customer. When she saw her mother come into the diner, she spun around and went to the kitchen. She pulled the cell phone out of her pocket.

"Hey babe, that was quick. Are you alone?" Jay answered.

"I need you to come over here now," she whispered.

"I'm on my way."

It surprised her that he didn't ask any questions. He didn't want to know what happened. It made her feel warm and for just a second, she smiled.

Harry looked at her from the grill. "Are you all right, Kate? You're a little pale."

She looked at him. "Remember the situation I told you about earlier? My mother just walked in the front door. Jay's on his way over from the rink. It will be all right when he gets here."

"Is that brassy blond out there your mom?"

"Yes. I should call Frank, too." She hit another button on the phone. After three rings, Frank picked up and she explained what new problem had developed.

Frank asked Kate to make sure Jay didn't kill anybody and said he would be on his way to the diner in a few minutes. Harry pointed at the door and said Jay arrived.

Kate walked out of the kitchen and stood at the end of the counter with her cell phone held tightly to her chest. She saw Jay stroll up to the table and heard her mother ask who the hell he was and what did he want.

He grinned a little maniacally and leaned over to give her a half hug. "I'm going to be your son-in-law, Mom. It's really good to meet you." He let her go and walked over to the man who sat across from the blond woman. "And you," he said and pointed at the guy. "I don't have a clue who you are, but it would be a good idea for you to stay seated. Unless your plan is to leave, then you can get up."

Kate put her hand over her mouth and tried not to laugh. The look on her mother's face was a priceless combination of surprise and disgust. She admired Jay. He was fearless and very brave and she wished she felt that way, too. She found him so attractive at that exact moment and wanted to take him into the locker room and show him how much he meant to her.

She looked at the couple that sat at the other table. They watched Jay's performance and then the man scooted his chair back and stood up. He took the woman he was with by the hand and led her out of the diner. *Lost business, damn*, Kate thought. She looked over her shoulder and saw Harry at the pass through window.

"That order's toast," he said and took the ticket off the wheel. "No worries."

****

"Now." Jay turned a chair around and sat down with his arms over the back. "If you're planning on dinner, Harry makes a great Mushroom-Swiss burger, but I think you should know that I've called the sheriff and he's on his way. Oh, and I'm a retired hockey player, so I love a good fight." He looked at the other man and smiled, again. "I'm sure you saw what I did to your little friend and, really, he is pretty scrawny, but he put his hand on my fiancée, which I can't deal with. It makes me very jealous if anyone, other than me, touches her." He looked back at her mother. "Do you understand where I'm coming from?"

Kate's mom frowned and looked at him with pinched lips. "I believe I do. I suppose the attorney is on his way, too?"

"I didn't call Frank," Jay said and looked at Kate. "Sweetheart, did you call Frank?" She nodded. "It looks like he's coming for the party, too."

"Mr...?" Kate's mom asked.

"Jason Hager, Mom, but everyone calls me Jay." He reached his hand over to shake, but when she rejected it, he just laughed.

"Mr. Hager, all I want is to speak to my daughter. This over-blown baboon act you're putting on is really unnecessary."

"Ah, now, Mrs. Douglas, we're getting started on the wrong foot."

"My name is Hardy, not Douglas."

He heard the bell on the door and felt a hand on his shoulder. When he looked up, he saw Frank and the Canon City sheriff. "Well, Mom, we'll have to get better acquainted on another day. You talk to the attorney." He stood up and walked over to Kate. He followed her through the swinging doors into the kitchen.

She turned and fell into his arms. He held her tight and could feel her shake, but realized she laughed.

Harry smiled at him from the grill. "Jay, you should take that performance on the road. You'd make a mint," he said and flipped a burger.

Jay felt Kate pull back and realized her hands were moving up his chest. She wrapped her arms around his neck and kissed his lips and face.

"My hero, you are too wonderful." She pulled up on her tip-toes to his ear and whispered, "I'll have to show you my appreciation later and it will be extra-special." She kissed him again and lowered back down. "I don't think I'm just falling in love anymore." She looked up at him and he put a hand on the back of her neck. He loved her beautiful blue eyes.

"What?" He realized he wasn't sure what she'd said.

"I am definitely in love with you." She hugged him and then pulled back again. "Hey, since when are we engaged?" she whispered.

"Sorry about that, I got a little ahead of myself. We haven't reached that part yet, but I'm pretty sure we will." He leaned in and took full control of her lips.

"Okay, you guys...Give the smooching for a rest a minute."

Jay pulled back from her and saw Frank and Sheriff Bennett walk into the kitchen. He saw Frank shake his head.

"That woman is a piece of work. She says she came here with no malice about the situation and only wants to talk to you, Kate. I said that you weren't going to speak with her alone. Tomorrow we're going to file the restraining order. It's up to you, Kate. If you say no, the sheriff will see her out of the diner and back to her car."

Jay felt her eyes on him as she looked up. "She scares the crap out of me, but I am a little curious about what she wants to say."

"You're sure you want to do this?" he asked and tightened his hold on her waist.

"You guys will all be there, right?"

Frank nodded. "Harry, maybe you should close up. I wouldn't want anyone to walk in on this conversation."

Harry started toward the swinging doors and Kate grabbed his arm. "Thank you, boss."

He patted her and went out to close the front. Fortunately, it had turned into a quiet night.

Kate looked up at Jay, again. "From the fat into the fire, right?"

"I'm right here with you." He leaned over and kissed her forehead.

"Okay then, let's get this over with." She walked out of the kitchen.

****

Kate moved around the counter and approached her mother's table. Jay followed right behind her and she could feel his presence which gave her a bit of calmness.

"There you are with your trained guard dogs," her mom said with a sarcastic grin.

"If that's the way you want to start this off, Edna, then we're dead in the water. You can criticize me all you want, but if you start on Jay and Frank, then we're done."

Her mom held up her hand. "Enough. I'm not here to argue. I just want one question answered. When are you going to give up this long road trip you've been on and come home?"

"Why are you going by Hardy?" Kate crossed her arms and stared at her mother. She ignored the question. Right now, Canon City sort of felt like home and Kate hoped she could make it stay that way for a very long time.

"Stacy..."

"I don't go by Stacy anymore, Edna."

"That's right, you're Kate now. Your father passed away about three years ago. He suffered a massive heart attack. I think his heart was broken when you ran off."

"Oh please, if he'd cared at all about me, he would have stopped you, when you took me from Portland to Colorado Springs."

"I've since re-married and you have a step-father."

"Tell me it was the asshole Jay popped in the nose yesterday."

"No, Max didn't come on this trip. He's still in Los Angeles. When he saw pictures of you and your long legs, he thought you'd be great in one of his films."

Kate heard the man who sat at the same table with her mother snort and laugh. Her mother gave the guy a look of disapproval.

"Max is a producer and is very certain he could get you some parts."

"I'm not an actress, Edna, and never will be. Is that all?"

"Sta...Kate, I haven't seen you for eight years and think we should get caught up," her mother said and leaned forward in her seat.

Kate again thought her mother looked like a snake, ready to pounce. "I don't see any need to get caught up and have nothing further to say to you. Stay away from me, Edna. Leave Canon City and forget about me. I don't know you and I'm not going to waste another minute trying to figure you out." She shrugged and turned to walk away. Jay held out his hand and she grasped it and followed him to the end of the counter.

He kissed her ear and whispered, "That was very well said, babe."

"She pisses me off," Kate whispered back.

Edna stood up from the table and looked angry. "Stacy, I am your mother and I deserve your respect and full attention. You can at least give me that."

Kate looked at the woman who thought she'd given so much and didn't seem to have a clue what she'd done to her child. It made Kate sick at her stomach. "Did I ever deserve your respect, *Mother*?" She voiced a heavy amount of sarcasm. "Did you ever once care what happened to me? Did you ever once care what David Farnsworth did to me? Or Jack Collins, my terrific coach, who beat me if I didn't skate his way? Didn't you ever wonder about the black eyes? Did you once believe it wasn't my fault that I broke three ribs and had to withdraw from Nationals?" She stepped in front of Jay and her hands were fisted at her sides. Somewhere in her gut, anger began to boil. Her voice got louder than she remembered it ever being with anyone and she felt rather proud of herself.

"Of course, it wasn't your fault. What Jack did screwed up your Olympic chances..."

"No, Edna. The Olympics weren't for another year. You came to my hospital room and said I needed to pay attention to what Jack told me to do and stop showing off. The creep almost killed me and you kept him as my coach. Was he a good fuck, Edna?"

"I never..." Her mother looked at her shocked and her face turned red.

"Yeah, you did. I saw you in Jack's car at the regional's in Phoenix. Your head in his lap and it moved up and down. Hmm...I wonder what you were doing? Did you do that for David, too? He sure liked it when I sucked him off." Kate looked at Jay, Frank and the sheriff and saw they all wore uncomfortable expressions on their faces. "Sorry, guys."

"I can see all your time alone on the road has turned your mouth into a trash heap. You need to clean that up, Stacy!" her mother snapped.

"I think this has gone far enough," Frank said and stepped between the two women. "Mrs. Hardy, there's nothing here to be gained. Go back to the rock you slithered out from under. If you contact my client again, you'll get a boat load of problems, particularly here in Canon City. Harry." Frank turned to the owner of the diner. "Kate is off the rest of the night. I hope that won't be a problem."

"No problem. I'm closed now anyway." Harry smiled.

"Sheriff Bennett, would you please see Mrs. Hardy and her friend to their car?"

The sheriff walked toward Kate's mother.

"You can't do that," Edna said.

"No, he can't, but I can." The sheriff pointed to the door. He put his hand on her elbow and started to pull her away from the table.

Kate watched her mother tug her arm away from the sheriff and move to the front door. She turned and looked Kate in the eye. "This isn't over, my daughter."

"I think it is," Frank said. After they left the room, Frank turned to Kate and took her hand. "Are you okay?"

"I will be." She'd gone back to feeling numb. She took her hand from Frank and clasped it in front of her. Even with Jay's hand on her shoulder, she felt very shaky. She knew he'd be able to tell, but at the moment it didn't matter. Even though she felt scared to death, she did feel good that she'd told her mother off. "I can't believe what just came out of my mouth," she said.

"Okay. Jay, please take Miss Beck home and treat her good or I'll kick your butt." Frank's attempt to lighten the mood fell flat. He looked at them. "Kate, everything is going to be all right. I promise that."

"You said the other day you didn't want to make promises you weren't sure you could keep." She looked up at him.

"Yeah, I did say that, but I feel we've got a pretty good harassment suit now and I have two witnesses, Harry and Sheriff Bennett. I'm sure they'd be willing to testify on your behalf."

Jay leaned over her and said, "Go get your coat, babe."

She looked up at him and smiled. For some reason she couldn't figure out, she felt good, but also uneasy. As much as she wanted it all to go away with her mother, she knew this was only the start.

Chapter Fourteen

Kate looked up at Jay as they stood at the corner and waited for the light to change so they could cross. They were headed back to the rink to get his Jeep.

"Jay, I want to skate."

"You got it, babe."

They turned around and headed to her apartment. She changed into a pair of faded jeans with holes in the knees and a gray sweatshirt. She pulled her skates out of the closet and opened the box. She went to a drawer in her dresser and found a pair of black gloves and a CD which she put in her purse.

When they got back to the rink, Kate sat down on the floor and started doing warm ups. Jay got her a bottle of water and his skates. She felt him watch her as she stretched the muscles in her legs and back. She sat up with her legs out to her sides and saw him look around the ice. He waved at the security guard, who stood near the other end of the ice and walked over to the boards to talk to the man. She heard Jay ask the guy to clean the ice.

After twenty minutes on the floor, Kate got up and put on her skates. She opened her purse and pulled the CD out. She put it into Jay's hand. "Can you put this on and play it loud?"

"Done," he said and ran up to the control booth.

When he came back down, Kate watched him walk toward her and smiled. "Jay?" She moved over to him on her skates and grabbed the shirt he wore. She put her lips on his and pulled back. She looked him in the eye and ran her fingers through his hair. "I love you and I'm so thankful we met. You are something I never dared dream of, but somehow all of my dreams are coming true."

He put his hands around her waist and held her tight. She heard the engine on the Zamboni turn off and Jay kissed her. "I'll be right back. It's time to get the music going."

Kate took her gloves out of her purse and slipped them on. She walked over to the ice and knelt down putting her gloved hand on it. She said the prayer and patted the ice and then stood back up. She heard Jay's voice on the speakers asking her to let him know when she felt ready to go. She took the blade guards off, stepped onto the ice and skated around once, then stopped in the middle. She looked up at the booth and gave him a thumbs-up.

After a few seconds the music she'd skated to so long ago started to play. She wasn't sure if she could remember the whole routine, but it didn't matter. She just wanted to feel the freedom she'd once felt whenever she skated her own style.

The music started out slow. She moved gently around the center before she broke off and headed down the ice. She did a spread eagle, spun around at the end, and then picked up speed as she moved to the other end of the ice. She felt it was the right pace, kicked her leg up and did the triple axel. After she landed she let her body flow with the gentle whistle from a flute. She realized she probably wouldn't be able to do the whole four minutes since her lungs started to hurt, but would go as far as she could.

She did a spiral, crossed over center ice and picked up speed again. The music began to pick up and got louder. After she did a couple of outside edge turns, she dropped into a sit spin, When she came up she did three twizzles on her left foot and then three on her right. Kate could feel her chest burn and knew she wouldn't finish.

She slowed her pace below the tempo of the music and bent at the waist. She put her hands on her knees. Over the music, she could hear Jay ask if she was okay. She straightened up and saw he sat on the boards at the other end. She skated down to him, moved her hands up his thighs and then wrapped her arms around his waist.

"You know what?" she asked, out of breath. She looked up into his warm brown eyes and started to melt. "You're mine, babe," she quoted his ringtone. "Put your skates on. I don't like being so far away from you."

"Yes, ma'am."

She slowly skated around the ice and listened to the music. It changed to another piece she'd used for a two minute program. It wasn't her favorite and she knew there were better pieces on the CD coming up that she liked better. She tried to do straight line steps, but found her edges were off and the blades probably needed to be sharpened. She did another couple twizzles and then a scratch spin.

When she stopped she saw Jay take off his blade guards and skate straight toward her. With his arms out he scooped her off her skates and she wrapped her legs around his waist.

****

She leaned in and kissed him. "I've never skated with a partner before."

"Neither have I. This is kind of different, but I like it. What were those spins you were doing on one foot?" He moved around the ice.

"They're called twizzles."

"I thought those were only done by the ice dancers?"

"Look at you, smart guy." She kissed his jaw. "That's where those spins are used the most, I guess. Single skaters can do them, too."

"Why are they different than sit spins or scratch spins?" He turned a corner and headed back down the ice.

"Twizzles can move across the ice, those other spins are supposed to stay in the same spot."

Jay let her down and they moved around the ice together. When Kate got her wind back, she broke off and did a Lutz jump and then a camel spin. Jay stopped by the boards and watched her skate. It amazed him how smooth she glided over the ice. At one point, she did a jump and almost landed on her butt. She corrected her footing quickly and got straightened up. He pushed off and caught up with her, pulling her back into his arms.

"I like you better this way." He moved to the far end board and sat her down on it. He stayed between her legs, put both hands in her hair and devoured her mouth. He hadn't meant to be so forceful, but couldn't hold back. They sucked each other's lips and when he put his hand on her breast, he felt her move her hand down the front of his pants and cup his penis with her fingers.

He moved his head back and was out of breath. "Babe, we need to go home."

"I agree."

He lifted her off the boards and they skated to the entrance. "I like your music. I got excited when you moved so smoothly to it. You really are graceful out there."

"Thank you." She smiled at him. "That compliment is better than any gold medal."

"Did you get enough skating time? I'm not making you quit too soon?" Jay asked and put on his blade guards.

"No, that's enough for tonight," she said. He saw her look out at the ice and could detect something that appeared to be longing in her eyes. "I may want to start doing this regular time though. Its good exercise and my lungs could use the workout."

"Do you sort of miss it, the skating and the attention?" he asked as they sat down at the table. He started to untie his skates.

She sat back in her chair. "Not so much the attention." She crinkled her nose and looked at him. "I think I just miss the freedom. I can't explain it, but

I get this emotional high when I'm out there and everything feels right."

Jay nodded. "I think I know what you mean. There's something about the movement on the ice that grabs at your head and...I don't know, it's sort of peaceful."

"Yeah, I suppose it has to do with a chemical reaction. I can't remember the word for that hormone that gets released, but when I skate it's such a good feeling."

****

As they finished changing back into their shoes, Jay looked at her. "Kate, have you ever thought about teaching?"

"No, not really."

"I can understand the parent issue better now since meeting your mom, but I think you'd be a great teacher."

"I'll think about it." She put her skates into the box and took off her gloves.

"I'll go get the CD and we'll be off." He stood up and held his skates by the laces.

She watched him turn and move to the stairs. She looked out at the ice again and thought maybe teaching wouldn't be so bad. She could start with just one or two kids. She refused to teach Shelby if it meant she'd have to deal with Monica. She'd probably be arrested for hitting that woman. Kate felt his warm hand on her shoulder.

"Ready?" he asked.

"Jay?" She stood up and looked up at him. "You do know I'm jealous of you."

"Jealous? Of what?"

"The relationship you have with your mom and dad." Kate's eyes started to fill, but she was determined not to cry and closed her eyes. She hated when she felt sorry for herself. "I never experienced what you have with your folks."

"What do you mean?"

"The way your mom teased you about the blood sacrifices still makes me laugh. I just am jealous that I don't know what that type of relationship feels like."

"I did tell you, my mom has your new cell phone number. On your next day off, I have a feeling you're going to be busy. She said something about cooking, shopping and lunch out. She thinks we spend too much time together and it would be best to split us up for a couple of hours."

"She did offer to teach me how to cook." She leaned up against him. It was the first time in a couple of days she felt calm, but also felt tired and needed some sleep. "Your mom was very nice to me the other morning."

"Come on, sweetheart. Let's get out of here."

Chapter Fifteen

Edna Hardy sat on the bed in her dreary hotel room. The TV played, but she'd kept the volume down. A headache pulsed in her temples and she didn't want to throw up. That asshole sheriff stood in the parking lot of the diner until Ken took off in the SUV. She'd wanted to go back in and finish the argument with her spoiled daughter, but the sheriff stood there and just watched as they drove away.

She took her water glass off the nightstand and sipped. Her cell phone rang and she picked it up. She smirked when she saw the name on the reader box.

"Hi, honey," she answered and waited to hear her husband's voice.

"Sweetheart, how did your meeting with Stacy go?" His deep voice made her head vibrate.

"Not well. She has a boyfriend and he thinks he's a superhero. He's tall and very full of himself. I guess he once played hockey. He broke Bradley's nose and I'd like to have him arrested for assault. As far as Stacy goes, I'm at a loss. She isn't willing to listen."

"Did you make her realize how much money she could make if she were to appear in one of our films?" Max asked.

"I didn't get a chance to bring it up. Her attorney and a sheriff showed up. It got a little ugly for a moment and Stacy made some very rude accusations."

"Edna, why don't you let it go, for now? Let Stacy know about the deal, come home and give her some time to think about what she's missing. Surely she doesn't think there's much for her there in Podunk, USA?"

"No, Max. She owes me. She could have made a mint with Stars on Ice, but at this point I think the skating is history. She's gotten too old, but she's kept her body in very good shape and she'd be fabulous in the bondage film you've tossed around. After this evening, I'd love nothing more than to see her chained up and screwed fiercely by Mr. Nine-inch."

"Do you mean Darren?"

"Is that his name? I have a terrible time with names." She heard Max let out a heavy breath and felt nervous for just a moment. "She might need a little body upgrade. Her breasts could be bigger," she said and wanted this conversation to go her way. She would get her way or make his life a living Hell.

"Sweetheart, why don't you just take her?"

Edna sat up straight on the bed and realized her headache started to get better. Then she thought of Ken and Bradley not wanting to bend the law. "There's a problem there, Max. I mentioned that possibility to Ken and he insisted on being a law-abiding citizen. I guess since he and Brad have already experienced prison, they don't want to go there again."

"Hmm...is that right? I should speak with them about that attitude. They're in the wrong business to look at things that way." The line went silent and then she heard her husband sigh. "I may have some other less law friendly men who could get the job done. Let me ask you this, Edna, my darling. Is she worth the price I'd have to pay these two men?"

She bit her lip and grinned. "Definitely, honey. We could clean up with DVDs alone and if I know my daughter, she'd be incredible in some BDSM films, too."

"Is she a screamer?"

"I don't know from firsthand experience, but I'm willing to bet she's very vocal."

"All right, sweetheart. I'll let you know after I've instructed my two men. It should be tomorrow or the next day at the latest. I want this done and get you back home. My bed is very cold without you."

"I'll be waiting on pins and needles, Max. I love you," she said and clicked her phone off. She held the phone to her lips, grinned and thought *this is going to be fun.*

Chapter Sixteen

Jay lay next to Kate under the comforter on his bed. They'd just woken up and the sun shone through the bedroom window. Their legs were tangled together. They kissed and let their hands wander and then heard the doorbell ring.

"Dammit, we're busy. I say let's ignore it," Jay said and put his lips back on hers. He pushed her onto her back and ran his hand down her pelvis.

"You'll get no complaint from me, babe." She smiled and kissed his chin. She ran her tongue down his neck and then sucked in a breath as his fingers found her nice, warm spot and slid between her wet folds and into her channel.

Jay put his lips back on hers and their tongues touched. He felt his penis grow harder and then his cell phone rang. He growled deep in his chest. "I may have to kill somebody." He kissed her nose and brought his hand out from under the covers. He picked up his cell phone and looked at the reader. "It's Frank." He pushed a receive button. "Hey, we're busy."

"I knew you were here. Get out of bed and answer the door. I have some news."

Jay hung up and looked down at Kate. "He's at the door and says he has some news."

She nodded. "I guess we'd better get up then. I'm going to mark this page in our book, so when we come back we can pick up from where we left off."

Jay chuckled. "I don't want to get up, but yeah, hopefully Frank won't be all long-winded lawyer and then we can come back and I'll let you devour my body, beautiful woman." He kissed her again and let her get up.

While she washed her face, Jay put on his jeans and ran down to the front door. Frank walked in and carried a bag of bagels and his briefcase.

"Do you want coffee?" Jay asked and walked into the kitchen.

"Yes, please. I've been up all night." Frank sat at the table and rubbed his eyes. "I didn't want to go over this on the phone."

"You could have at least combed your hair and put on a clean shirt. You look like crap, man," Jay said and put coffee into the maker.

"Thanks, I'll remember that next time we're on the ice with our brooms."

"So, the news, is it good?" Jay turned from the coffee pot and looked at him. Frank glanced up at him and shook his head. "Are you trying to give me a heart attack?"

"No."

They heard Kate's footsteps come down the stairs. Jay poured water into the coffee maker and tried not to get worried. When he turned back around, Kate entered the kitchen and Frank stood up from his chair and smiled.

"Hi Frank. Please, sit down. It's too early in the day for formality," she said and walked to the other side of the table. Jay sat down next to her and took her hand.

"Early? It's ten o'clock." Frank eased himself back down. "How are you doing this morning, Kate?"

"I'm fine," she said. Jay thought he could hear tension in her voice. "Yesterday felt pretty intense, but you'll be pleased to know Jay took extremely good care of me last night as per your instructions." She smiled and leaned on Jay's shoulder.

"Good. I'm glad he listened to me for a change." Frank sat forward and put his hands on the table. "So, no time like the present, right? I have some good news and some weird news. I'm going to start with the weird. After that little meet over at Harry's Diner last night, something your mom said bugged me."

"Long legs," Jay said. He hoped and prayed it wasn't what he thought.

Frank looked at him. "You too?" Jay nodded.

"Did I miss something?" Kate looked back and forth between them.

"No, it's a guy thing. When I got home last night, I got online and searched your new step-dad, Max Hardy." Frank sat back and crossed his arms over his chest.

Jay saw a frown on Frank's face and thought he looked in pain. "What did you find out?"

Frank huffed and looked away from them. "I said it yesterday, Kate. Your mother is a piece of work. Max Hardy does make films, but not the reputable kind."

"Porn?" Jay asked and watched Frank nod. "Son-of-a-bitch."

Kate sat forward and let go of Jay's hand. "Frank, are you saying she wants me for porn films?"

"Direct to DVD and it's a very lucrative business. Max Hardy is one of the biggest names in that business and yes, I believe that's why they're after you."

The room went dead silent, except for the gurgle from the coffee maker. Jay felt a weight land on his shoulders and he wasn't sure what he should do first. Did he need to hold Kate and comfort her or go find her mother and give her a piece of his mind? He felt torn between worry and anger.

Kate sat back and pinched her nose with fingers. "Unbelievable. You were right, Frank. This is weird."

"Max Hardy DVD's can be really brutal. I read there isn't any form of sex he hasn't touched on in his little films. Bondage, bestiality, orgies, you name it and he'll film it. The one thing, Kate, is that your mother never came right out and said that's what they're after. She never said she wants you for porn films, but when you hear the good news it will have to make you wonder."

Jay stood up and pulled the cabinet door open. He took three mugs out and slammed the door shut. He poured three cups of coffee and took them to the table. When he sat back down, he saw Frank watched him. "What?" he asked.

"I know your pissed, Jay. Tone it down, okay. I've said it before; I don't want to have to defend you right now."

Jay nodded and put his arm around Kate's shoulders. "So what is the good news?"

Frank looked at Kate. "Your dad is alive. Your mother divorced him three years ago, but he's alive and well in Portland. I got in touch with him this morning and he wants to talk to you, Kate. I'm supposed to call him later and let him know if you'll agree to see him. Your dad says he can get a flight and be here by tomorrow. The fact that your mother lied about him being dead makes me wonder about her motivations. I think she wants you for the money that can be made off the films. I doubt she'd come right out and admit it, but that's what I believe."

"And that's all she wants me for is the money. That's what you're saying?" Kate said.

"That's what I truly believe." Frank nodded.

Jay tried to take her hand, but she pushed him away. She stood up and stared at Frank. She started to say something, but stopped and left the table.

Jay watched her head to the living-room. "Frank, how about I call you later. You can take the coffee with you."

"I brought bagels," Frank said and looked at Jay. He nodded. "We still need to discuss which subject to focus on first. Go to her and we'll enjoy breakfast after a bit."

Jay got up and followed Kate. He saw the doors to the deck open and she stood at the rail, her hands tightly held onto the wooden post. He could see white spots on her knuckles.

"Babe." He stood next to her, but didn't touch her.

"Jay," she said and her voice cracked. "Remember when we ate lunch a couple of weeks ago? I told you when things get too close, it's time for me to leave. And sometime later you said if I felt panicked I should let you know and we'd talk about it? " She looked up at him as a tear rolled down her cheek.

Jay felt scared. Her eyes looked angry and hard, but tears ran from them. He could tell she was hurt and wanted to hold her. As he reached up to touch her cheek, she moved back a step. He dropped his hand. "Fine, we'll both go. Give me half an hour to pack up some stuff. We'll take the Jeep and head out."

"That's really nice of you, but no. I wanted too much. I felt lonely and thought maybe I could have a normal relationship, but..." She looked away from him at the back yard. "I don't think it's in my cards to ever be happy. For some reason the Gods are against me. You can't leave, Jay. You have family and friends here and you'd only end up hating me for taking you away."

Jay moved up to her and put one hand behind her neck. The other slid around her waist. She tried to push him away, but he pulled her close and rested his head on her shoulder.

"In case you hadn't noticed, Kate, I can't live without you now and if it means we leave together, then so be it."

Kate stopped trying to push him away and he straightened. He saw her frown and her eyebrows folded together. "Jay, why are you shaking?"

"You're scaring the crap out of me, sweetheart. I find someone for the first time in my life and for some crazy cosmic reason I love her more than anything and because of outside troubles she's threatening to disappear from my life. I can understand how people sometimes go completely mad and do terrible things, because if I don't leave with you that might be me. I seriously want to hurt your mother. Sweetheart, please, let me help you fight her."

Kate put her hand on his chest. He let go of her neck and put his hand over hers. "Jay, think what this will mean for you. I can't ask you to do this," she said.

"Babe, don't make me strap you down with duct tape and keep you captive." He moved his hands down her shoulders and held onto her upper arms.

She looked at him and her frown got deeper. "This is not funny, Jay, and you said you weren't into bondage." She hit him on the shoulder.

"Are you pissed at me?"

"Yes."

"Good, hold that feeling and let me help." He looked into her eyes and knew she was confused.

"Excuse me," Frank said from the door. "I'm not sure about the duct tape thing, but I want to help, too. Kate, you've got to know if Jay's begging then I think you're going to have a hard time getting rid of him."

Jay watched her expression soften and she grabbed onto his shirt.

"I need to think. I'm going to take a shower." She looked up at him.

"Can I join you?" Jay asked and kept hold of her arms.

"No, I need some space for a little while. Talk to Frank and drink too much coffee." She let go of his shirt and walked into the house.

****

Kate let the hot water pound onto her neck and shoulders. She wanted to scream, cry, beat up on something and laugh hysterically all at once. She placed her hands on the tiles and put her head down between her arms. The warm water moved down her back and legs and helped with the chill that over took her. A voice kept a litany going in her brain. Over and over it said the time had come to find a bus out of Colorado. It stabbed at her heart to think she might hurt Jay. The thought of him leaving Canon City with her was impossible. He'd been so kind to offer, but she couldn't ask him to give up his life.

She put her head on her arm on the shower wall. Besides her brain telling her to leave, it screamed at her about her mother's lies. That woman's lies affected her life for far too long and she felt angry at herself for being scared. She'd let everything her mother said make her feel small, afraid and vulnerable.

She turned off the water, dried off and got dressed. She used Jay's hair dryer and brush and looked at herself in the mirror. There she saw a woman who didn't want to run anymore. She was tired and wanted a life. She wanted to be a part of something and not be on the outside anymore. She felt sick of watching people around her enjoy their lives.

Kate put her socks on and went down the stairs. Jay and Frank still sat at the kitchen table. They'd torn open Franks bag of bagels and prepared them, but neither man had touched the food. She walked over to Jay and wrapped her arms around his shoulders. She kissed his neck and sat down next to him.

"Do you want some coffee, babe?" Jay asked.

"No, not right now." She wove her fingers through his and put their hands on her lap. "I've made a decision." Jay and Frank both looked at her expectantly. "Frank, would you call my dad and tell him I've got my hands full with my mother. Tell him when she's gone, I'll think more seriously about contacting him."

"Got it," Frank said.

"So, other than killing my mother and burying the body up in the mountains, how do I get rid of her?"

"I can have my assistant file the restraining order today. It will keep her at least one thousand feet away from you. I've also got papers ready for a harassment suit. We can threaten her with it and ask for an ungodly amount of mental compensation."

"Frank, the only thing I want from her is to never see her again. I know we're supposed to forgive, but it's going to be a really long time, if ever, before that happens. Even if we won against her, I don't want money. I just want her to agree never to step near me again." Kate stood up and went to the coffee maker. She found the cups and poured. "Wait a minute, I had a cup of coffee..."

"It got cold, babe. I cleaned the cup and put it away."

She nodded and carried the new cup to the table.

"Kate, I contacted Harry and let him know, again, you won't be at work tonight and will probably be out the rest of the week. He said not to worry, your job is safe," Frank said. "I'm going to set up a meeting with your mother as soon as we can."

"Frank, is there any way you could have this conference without me? It makes me so uncomfortable to be around her and I'd rather not attend." The last thing she wanted was to deal with her mother. A plan started to form in her head, but she didn't have it complete yet. She knew there was only one answer to her problem.

"We need to do this. If we face her head on, you'll be finished with her forever and can look to the future. If we don't get the ball rolling, you'll still be looking over your shoulder and I know you don't want that, sweetheart," Frank said.

"Okay then let's do it. The sooner the better." She took a sip of coffee and then looked at both of them. Her eyes settled on Jay. "I want to run. I think it's ingrained into my genes. It's really hard not to go and pack my bag." She looked at his eyes and put her hand on his cheek.

"Are you two certain you don't want to use my cabin for a few days?" Frank asked.

"That's very nice, but I've decided not to run. My head still wants to go to the bus station and get out of Colorado." She ran her thumb over Jay's lips and leaned over to kiss him. "I want to fight it as much as possible. I think what Jay and I have is more important than any threats my mother can dish out. It's time I stopped being scared all the time and fight for what I want. Thank you for the offer, Frank."

"Jay, you're awfully quiet over there. Are you okay?"

Kate saw Jay look across the table at Frank and nod. "I'm just watching my woman stake her claim and enjoying every minute of it." Jay smiled and squeezed her hand.

Frank shook his head. "All right then, I've got some work to do and I'll contact you later with the time of the meeting." He put his bagel onto a napkin and stood up. "I'll see you later."

"Frank, get some rest. You look done in," Kate said and smiled.

They both said goodbye, but didn't leave the table and sat quietly for a few minutes. Kate finally turned sideways on her chair and put her feet on the crossbar of his.

"Jay, sweetheart, good-looking man, darling, dear...hmm, what other endearments can I use?" She put her hand on his shoulder.

He leaned on her knees. "How about scorching hot dude or luscious lips?"

"I did say good-looking man."

"Yeah, but I'm more than just *good*, right?"

Kate laughed and moved her hands around his neck. "Yeah, you are. Thank you for being so incredibly patient today. I still want to run, but the part that wants to fight for you - for us - has gotten a little bigger. Little bigger? I wonder if that's correct."

Jay took hold of her leg and started to pull it over his legs. He leaned over and grabbed her rear end. He pulled her onto his lap and kept his hands on her behind. "You were too far away from me. You're welcome." He moved his arms around her and gave her a tight hug.

"Babe, I can't guarantee I won't ever not want to run, but I can work on it and try to keep the panic under control. I just...I don't want..."

He let her sit up straight. "What?"

"I don't want you to get frustrated with me. It's got to be difficult for you to put up with all this crap. I'm so sorry to drag you into it."

He put his hands on either side of her face and looked into her eyes. "Kate, you are who you are and I don't expect you to change for me. The only thing I ask is that you don't push me away anymore and don't run. That hurts my heart more than anything. We can get this worked out."

"That's two things, Jay." She put her hand on his cheek and kissed his lips. She felt his hands move back down to her waist and then up under her shirt.

"You're right. How can you stand a boyfriend who can't even count?"

"I'll have to suffer." She licked his lip and put hers fully on his. She swept her tongue over his, around his teeth and brushed his top lip and sucked it.

"Babe, before we digress into two overly horny people I just want to make sure we're okay. I need to know you're really going to stay and not run." He looked up at her.

Kate gazed at his brown eyes and heard the overwhelming need in his voice. "Yeah, we're good and I'm not going anywhere."

"Okay. Good." He smiled. "This shirt needs to come off then." He kissed her. "Please."

"Oh, all right. If you insist." She pulled the shirt off and unhooked her bra. She sighed as his hands moved along her sides to frame her breasts. "I do love the way you touch me," she said as his fingers moved over her nipple and he kissed her shoulder.

"I love you so much, Kate. You do know that, right?"

"Yeah, I know. I love you, too."

She saw his eyes go down to her chest and he grinned. "Babe, you are so beautiful. I hope you don't have any plans this afternoon. I think we're going to be very busy." He looked up at her. "We'll most likely need to take another shower."

Chapter Seventeen

They spent the rest of the day relaxed and lazy. Kate tried to get Jay to go into the rink, but he didn't want to leave her. As much as she guaranteed she wouldn't run, she could tell he had a hard time letting go of what he felt. She was glad that they were honest with each other about the relationship. He did apologize to her and said he worried that she might feel he didn't trust her not to run. Kate understood that she hadn't given him much of a reason to trust her for not disappearing. Since they'd only known each other a couple of weeks, they agreed they still had a lot to learn about one another.

In the evening, they went to a Chinese restaurant and ordered take-out. They brought it back to his house and watched a movie while they ate broccoli beef, almond chicken and fried rice. When Kate broke open a fortune cookie the note inside said, *You will get all you desire*. This caused her to cry and another long discussion started about hope.

Jay told her to think positively and remember the good guys always win.

Kate knew that what she wanted to do was going to be very difficult. Guilt stabbed at her heart because she felt sure if she went through with her plan, Jay would no longer be a part of her life. She didn't have a clue if she could pull it off, but would have to wait for the right time.

"Jay, tell me some good tips to deal with my mother." Kate lay on her side and moved her hand on his chest.

"What do you mean?" He put his hand over hers and then kissed her palm.

She propped up on her elbow and looked down at him. "At the diner, I started the discussion with her and felt sort of indifferent. It really didn't matter to me what she thought, but by the end I was scared again."

"Right, your mom pushed at your emotional buttons and played a guilt card or tried to."

"What do you mean?"

"That business about not respecting her...when we're kids we usually are brought up and taught, *thou shalt love thy mother and father*, but these days if parents treat the kids bad, how can the kids be expected to respect them? So, if your mom tries to push your guilt button, don't let her. Remember how mad you are about the way she hasn't respected you. She can threaten all she wants, but it's just her way to feel superior over you. She gets off on it. I know it's easier said than done, but just ignore her."

"Jay, did you just quote the Ten Commandments?"

"Yeah, I went to Sunday school and everything, when I was little," he said with a sing-song voice.

"You're a smart, scorching hot man." She put her head back on his chest.

"Not so smart. I have a hard time writing complete sentences and I don't even want to talk about math. My accountant double checks my numbers every month." He rolled her onto her back and kissed her neck. "Would you like to do a skate around tonight?"

"I don't know. I'm full of fried rice and I like the peace I'm experiencing right now." She smiled at him. "It would also mean I have to get up and get dressed. I just want to hold you right now."

"Then we'll stay put and I'll worship your body some more." He leaned toward her and brushed her lips. "Why do you have such a huge grin on your face?"

"You crack me up sometimes. Worship my body?" She laughed.

"Hey, in case you hadn't noticed" - he moved down a little and cupped her breast with his hand - "I'm totally addicted to your breasts. They're better than drugs any day of the week. They make me high, but I can still drive and don't get a hangover."

She continued to laugh and tried to turn on her side, but Jay pinned her down. His lips kissed the soft skin on one of her breasts and caused her to moan.

They heard his phone ring and quieted down. Jay's head popped up and he frowned. "Damn, it never fails." He reached for the phone and looked at the screen. "It's Frank." He hit the receive button. "Hey. What's up?"

Kate looked up at him and could hear Frank's voice, but it sounded like a squeaky toy.

"Okay...yep, tomorrow. We'll be there. Good." He clicked the phone off and put it on the nightstand. "We have a meeting tomorrow at 11:00 o'clock."

"With her?" She saw him nod. "Why doesn't she just let it go?" She frowned.

"Sweetheart, maybe we'll find out tomorrow what she wants and then inform her you're not leaving Canon City."

"Great and we get another night's lost sleep."

"A few years ago, I read a self-help book to deal with some anger issues."

"You read a self-help book? Wow, you are smart."

"A woman I was involved with cheated on me and lied about it. She also became pregnant and tried to pin it on me, but I wasn't the father. I felt so pissed, but needed to keep it under control. This book gave some advice about other issues besides anger, one of which was that tomorrow is tomorrow. Why let it bother you today, when tomorrow could be completely different than what you'd worried about? It could be different and you'd worried about it for nothing."

"I guess that makes sense." She moved her hands over his shoulders and saw his lips curve up softly.

"Just remember how pissed you are with her and keep her away from your buttons?"

Kate pushed up and kissed him. "You're the only one I allow anywhere near my buttons. I like how you push them and I have my own addiction." She moved her finger over his lips.

"Oh yeah?"

"Yeah, you have great lips and I love your tongue when it pushes my button." She arched her eyebrows and smiled. She felt warmth in her cheeks and knew she was blushing.

"I'll have to remember that the next time you're pissed at me." He moved his hand down to her pelvis and found her nib. "Ah, there's the button I was looking for."

"Hush up, Jay, and kiss me. I'm getting hot with you on top of me."

Kate did lose sleep that night. She'd just drop off and the nightmare would start. Her mother yelled at her and the coach would swing and hit her. It became difficult to close her eyes and she tossed and turned.

In the middle of the night, Kate got up and went downstairs. She tried to watch TV with the sound off, but she couldn't concentrate on the programs. It was also difficult to follow her book and after she read the same paragraph a few times, she set the book aside and wound up out on the deck.

The night felt cold, but it didn't seem to matter. She listened to the quiet and looked at the stars. *What would it be like someplace else?* That question went through her brain and made her sad. She didn't want to leave.

She thought about how hard Jay worked to protect her and the love that crawled through her for him grew stronger every day. The idea she'd come up with continued to play over and over in her brain and as much as she didn't like it, she knew to leave Canon City was her only answer. She knew deep in her heart that she'd never feel at peace if she stayed. Peace was such a nice word and she wanted to know what it felt like.

She'd put her head on her knees and didn't realize she'd fallen asleep. Nice warm hands picked her up and she became aware she moved.

"I'm sorry, Jay. I couldn't sleep and didn't want to wake you," she mumbled against his chest.

"It's all right, sweetheart." He set her on the bed and covered her with the quilt.

She felt him slide in next to her and wrap his arms around her body.

"Try to get some rest. I won't let anything hurt you. I promise," he whispered in her ear.

Chapter Eighteen

Kate and Jay walked into Frank's office hand in hand, dressed casually in jeans. She wore her purple fleece sweater for luck and Jay wore his University of Colorado sweatshirt. She felt a little embarrassed that she didn't have a nicer outfit to wear, but she'd stayed away from buying a lot of extra clothes in the past, due to the need to run fast from any given situation.

Frank came out of his office and waved them in. Kate tried not to be scared, but she'd slept very little the night before and felt tired. After Jay found her on the porch they'd talked almost until sunup and he'd tried to get her to feel calm, but she just couldn't get her brain to shut up.

Frank asked them if they wanted coffee, but both declined. "Okay, first of all, Kate you are now legally Kathryn Beck. Here are your papers." He handed her a folder. "You can look them over later. Tomorrow or in the next couple of days you'll need to go over to DMV to get a Colorado State identification card. We need you on record as a resident of the state. In the folder you'll find a photocopy of your birth certificate. It's under your original name, but the other papers are notice of the legal change. You'll want to keep them together." He sat back in his chair. "Now, the only other development is that the restraining order was served yesterday. As I'm sure you can guess, your mother is pissed about it. Too bad for her." He smiled.

Kate nodded and smiled a little, but her gut tightened.

"Your mother is also not happy about the lawsuit, but since we have a statement from a senior police officer and Harry about their harassment at the diner, I think she realizes if it goes to trial she won't have a leg to stand on. Sweetheart, you have a funny expression on your face."

She looked at Frank and tried to smile. "I just keep waiting for the other shoe to drop," Kate said.

"There is no other shoe at this point. Listen to me, you're twenty-five-years-old and she has no parental control over you. I want you to be able to have a normal life and if she keeps shadowing you it amounts to harassment. I'd love to slap her with a stalking lawsuit, but hope we can get rid of her this way. If she wants to threaten, we can threaten back."

A woman came in through the door into the office and nodded. "They're here, Frank. I put them in conference room ten. She has an attorney with her."

"Woo...I'm scared. It's probably some over-priced Los Angeles idiot. This should be fun." Frank stood up and tightened an invisible tie around his neck. He did wear nicer slacks, but it occurred to Kate that she'd never seen him with a tie on. He pulled a jacket off his chair and slipped it on.

"Why don't you wear ties?" Kate asked.

"I've always hated those damn things. The last time I wore one was at high school graduation and I felt like I had a noose around my neck the whole time. Yuck."

"Frank, you are so weird sometimes," Jay said.

"Just because I hate ties, I'm weird? Kate, does that seem weird to you?" Frank looked at her and smiled. He tried to lighten the mood, she thought, but it didn't work. Her stomach felt like one large knot.

Kate looked at them both. "I plead the fifth."

"Very good." Frank walked around the desk and offered his arm to Kate. "Let's go kick some butt."

Kate walked down the hallway between Jay and Frank. The thought of walking into that room made the huge knot in her stomach start to burn and her heart pounded in her chest. She saw the two men that were her mother's assistants as they waited outside the conference room. The one that Jay punched wore two black eyes and looked like a raccoon.

Jay took her hand and laced his fingers through hers. All feeling went out of her feet and she felt weighed down, as though lead melted into her shoes. Kate looked up at him and tried to smile.

"What?" he asked, quietly.

"I just adore you like crazy," she said and tried to get her brain to brave up. She took in a breath and tried to settle the knot that seared in her stomach.

She felt eyes watch her as she sat down at the table. She glanced at her mother, whose mouth was pinched into a line. She turned her gaze to her hand which was held tightly in Jay's.

The two attorney's introduced one another. Edna's attorney, John Levine, had dark hair and eyes. He was tall, but portly with short, stumpy legs.

They began discussions about the terms of the restraining order. Kate tried to listen but her mind wandered. She knew, at this point, the woman across the table from her meant nothing. She thought she should feel something - guilt or sadness - about the way her emotions were toward her mother, but didn't feel anything like that. Kate was angry and still scared at all she could lose and remembered that Edna had no hold over her. That thought was the most important part of all this and she needed to keep her focus on it as much as possible. *No hold* became her mantra.

Edna stared across the table at her and, obviously, tried to intimidate Kate. It did work, but for a moment she realized she didn't care anymore and she felt her lips curl at the ends. She found that her stomach settled down a bit and the fear went down to a low simmer. She hated this woman and knew she'd probably never be rid of her, but it didn't matter. Kate's plan would work and she'd figured out the way to make it go.

Kate heard Frank say something about the harassment lawsuit and realized that it made no difference to her. She wanted nothing from Edna. She reached over to Frank and touched his arm. She stopped him mid-sentence and stared Edna in the eyes. Something shifted inside Kate, but she couldn't tell you what it was. Maybe pity or sympathy for her mother, maybe it was just nothing.

Kate stood up and placed both her hands flat on the table. "This is turning into a made for TV movie and it's ridiculous. Edna, you haven't been a part of my life for many, many years and I have no room for you now. My mother died eight years ago, in a hospital room in Portland and I have nothing left to me but you." She pointed across the table. "You're a shell, empty of any care or consideration of those around you. Are you even aware of how your actions affect other people? Go back to whatever life you're involved with, and just forget I exist. When I leave this room, I'll never think of you again. When you are old, I hope you die alone. Then you'll get a glimpse into the non-life I've led for the last eight years. I hope it will open your eyes and you will feel some regrets, but I doubt it. You are nothing to me." Kate moved her chair back and started out of the room.

She heard a voice shout at her and footsteps followed her as she went through the door. She looked at the two men who stood outside and shook her head. She kept her feet moving and when she got out of the building, she tipped her head up to feel the warmth from the sun on her face. She felt comforted by the warmth and for the first time in years, she'd become calm. She saw a bench on the sidewalk and went over to sit. The cars on the road went both directions and she wondered where they were off to. Jay sat next to her and took her hand in his.

"Jay, do you want children?" she asked and continued to watch the traffic move.

"Someday, maybe. Why?"

She turned on the bench and put her hand on his chest. "I swear to you, right here and now, I'm going to work very hard at never being like Edna. You have my permission, should I ever show signs of becoming a heartless woman, to lock me in a room and de-program me."

"I don't think that will ever be necessary, sweetheart. Unlike your mother, you are self aware and actually care how you treat other people."

"Let's go over to the rink. I think I'd like to volunteer my services to one of the teachers."

"You got it." He stood up and held out his hand, but just then Jay's cell phone started to ring. He looked at the screen. "It's Frank. Yep...yeah, we're outside on the side walk. Kate feels you can handle things just fine...she's nodding her head. Yep." Jay put the phone against his chest. "He wants to talk to you."

Kate took the phone. "Yes, Frank."

"Could we maybe finish this meeting before you and Jay disappear? I still need to determine if we're going to move forward with the suit and for that I need your signature, Miss Beck."

"I don't really want to see her anymore, like never."

"Kate, please come back inside," Frank said.

Kate looked up at Jay and smiled. "Frank said please. I'm such a sucker for good manners." Jay held her hand and they started to move back to the building. "Okay, Frank, you win this time."

When they walked back into the conference room, Edna looked at Kate and laughed.

"I see you're still running away, Stacy."

"Counselor, please instruct your client to keep her mouth shut. She needs to understand that the restraining order means no contact physically or verbally. She doesn't have anything to say that we wish to hear at this time," Frank said and looked angry.

Kate watched Frank and tried to adopt some of his anger, but didn't feel it. She just wanted to focus on her and Jay for as long as possible, nothing more.

"Mr. Donnelly, I'm her mother and I can say whatever I want to her."

Frank frowned at Edna and leaned on the table. "Not in this meeting, Mrs. Hardy. I'm sure you attorney has explained that to you."

Kate and Jay sat down again and she felt comfortable. She looked at Jay and smiled. His eyes grinned back at her and she wanted nothing more than to drown in his warmth and sweetness. She heard Frank start to speak again.

"We were discussing the restraining order which was signed by Judge David Soren. You may have no contact with Miss Beck..."

"You've said that already and her name isn't Beck. It's Stacy Hardy and if your records say anything else, then they are wrong," Edna snarled at him.

"Ma'am, her name was never Stacy Hardy," Frank commented and looked across the table curiously.

Kate saw her mother's grin snap to a frown in a heartbeat and wondered where that name entered the picture. She'd never even met her mother's new husband. She watched Frank hand a sheet of paper to the other attorney.

"This document sighed and witnessed in the state of Colorado, says, legally, her name is Kathryn Beck. Why did you call her Stacy Hardy?" Frank looked across the table at Edna.

"It was a slip of the tongue, Mr. Donnelly," Edna said and the other attorney leaned over and whispered something in her ear. "This is all so very upsetting..."

"By the end of business today, we will file the harassment papers and begin that lawsuit against your client. We are asking for a settlement of eight million dollars."

"Excuse me?" Edna shifted in her chair and looked uncomfortable. She peered at her attorney who glanced over the paperwork. "I don't know how you came up with that ludicrous amount, but she'll never see a dime of it. If anything she owes me," Edna snarled.

"It looks like they're serious Mrs. Hardy. I think the amount you've asked for is very unreasonable, Mr. Donnelly." Mr. Levine, the other attorney, wadded the paper in his hand and threw it on the floor.

"I take it that amount is not acceptable? Fine, we will raise it to ten million dollars, then."

"Mr. Donnelly, any amount is ridiculous." Mr. Levine looked at Edna and started to move his chair back.

"Fine, we will see you in court, perhaps by next winter." Frank smiled and started to stand up.

"Wait a minute." Edna held up her hand. "What can I do to make this go away?"

"You can leave Canon City and never contact my client again. If you default on that agreement then we will go ahead with the suit, and believe me there will be papers to sign which I will hold you to," Frank said.

"I will agree to that and sign the papers, but with one condition. I get to speak to my daughter for thirty minutes, alone. We don't need all this fucking testosterone in the room." Edna looked at Kate.

She looked up at Frank, who didn't move. She nodded.

"You'll get ten minutes and no more," he said.

"I'm not leaving Kate alone with that bitch," Jay snapped and pointed at Edna.

Kate felt his hand tighten on hers and looked at him. She leaned toward him and whispered in his ear, "It's okay, babe. She can't hurt me anymore."

Jay shook his head. "I don't like it," he whispered back.

"I know." She smiled at him and then looked at those around the table. "I have my own condition. The door stays open."

"So you can run again?" Edna smirked.

"No. It's so that Jay and Frank can stand in the hallway and hear what's said. I have no secrets from them and don't trust you at all."

"Mr. Levine will listen in then, too."

"That's fine with me." Kate slightly tilted her head and smiled.

Edna rolled her eyes and continued to smirk as the men stood up and started out of the room.

Jay leaned over Kate and kissed her cheek. "You're sure about this?" he asked and looked into her eyes.

"Don't go too far, okay? I'd like to be able to look at you out in the hallway." She rubbed his arm and melted into his eyes.

Kate stood up and watched Jay leave the room. He stood in the hallway where she could see him and she almost started to giggle like a school girl. She moved to the window and leaned against the sill. She looked across the table and did laugh. Jay called her mother a witch once and Kate thought he was right. All she needed was a broom and pointy hat and she'd be a perfect wicked witch. Edna leaned back in her chair and crossed her arms.

"Where's my father?" Kate asked.

"I told you he's dead."

"Which is a lie. He's very much alive."

"But, dead to me. Portland is such a nowhere town. I never understood why he wanted to live there. You know, he wants nothing to do with either of us, and particularly not you."

"That's another lie. Frank contacted him and he offered to catch the next plane out. Why do you feel all of the lies are so necessary, Edna?" Kate gripped the sill on either side of her and hoped she didn't peel the paint off with her fingernails. "I don't get it. You were born in Portland, why do you hate it so much?"

"There's nothing in that town for me. I want more and have it in Los Angeles with Max. You could have it, too, Stacy. That town really has so much to offer."

Kate just stared at her. "I'm not Stacy and I don't want what you offer. It isn't for me. I have all I need here in Canon City."

Edna stood up and walked to the end of the table. "I'm tired of your wasted life. You are only twenty-five and could be so much more than a waitress in this dumpy town."

"You mean, I could be a porn star?"

"There's a lot of money in it, sweetie, and you have a great body. Max says your legs alone would rake in the bucks. God, don't look at me like that, Stacy. It's just sex."

Kate couldn't believe the words that came out of this woman's mouth. "I'm sorry you feel that way, Edna, because I don't."

Her mother came up to her at the window, but Kate didn't move. She felt scared, but didn't want Edna to think she felt intimidated.

"I wonder what would happen to your little life if someone were to accuse your boy-toy of rape? Or maybe he abused one of his little hockey boys," Edna whispered and grinned at Kate.

Kate saw Jay come closer to the doorjamb. She knew he could tell by the look on her face that her mother said nothing good. "What?" She pushed away from the sill and stared at her mother. All of the strength she'd walked into the room with, sank into her shoes. Fear exploded back into her brain.

"Yeah, the little tramp that called me about you being here in Canon City...what was her name? Oh yes, Monica is more than willing to earn a few extra bucks. She could paint a very poor picture of how what's-his-name treats women and how he stalked her."

Kate continued to stare at her mother and felt her heart begin to pound. "You bitch." She started to move past Edna, who grabbed her wrist and pulled her close.

"You know me well enough, Stacy. You know I'll do it," she hissed. "He's nothing and it would ruin him completely. What would all those parents think if a rumor started about how he likes little boys? There's no life for you here. Nothing. You may as well get over it and give in. Come to Los Angeles with me and let me show you how to live."

Kate pulled her wrist out of Edna's hand. "I never thought I'd truly meet evil, but it stands right in front of me now. How could you do that, Edna and still sleep at night? Don't you have any heart, or is it rotted, like the rest of you?"

Jay and Frank, and her mother's attorney all came back into the room when Kate started to shout.

"This is finished, Kate," Frank said.

She didn't hear him and moved quickly to the door. She saw Jay as she passed him and he looked very concerned. She couldn't stop and kept moving to get away from the woman who claimed to be her mother.

Chapter Nineteen

When Kate got out the front door onto the sidewalk, she looked both ways and couldn't remember which way to go. She wanted to get to her apartment, pack her duffle bag and get to the bus terminal before anyone could find her.

She ran along the side of the busy four-lane road until the sidewalk ended and then heard gravel crunch under her feet. She saw a big truck come toward her on the inside lane and she felt ready to throw herself in front of it. If it would keep her mother from continuing this game she played, then Kate was willing to give up her life.

Cars whizzed past her and the air from them made her hair swirl as her feet continued to move. Another big truck headed her way in the closest lane and she started to move right, when a strong arm wrapped around her waist and pulled her off her feet. Her lungs burned and she tried to fight against his strength. Jay's arms were around her and he breathed hard, too.

"Let me go, Jay. Please, just let me leave. I refuse to deal with her anymore. It hurts too much and I can't take it." She tried to get out of his hold, but couldn't budge him. "She's never going to quit and leave me alone. I have to go." She saw a BMW pull up to the curb and Frank looked up at them.

Jay opened the back door and put her onto the seat. She squirmed out of his hold and tried to open the other door, but Frank had it secure locked. Jay pulled her away from the door, but she just went wild and hit at him.

"God, what? Now I'm your fucking prisoner? Let me go." she shouted and pushed away from him. She covered her face with her hands and continued to cry. "I know I promised not to run, but I can't take it anymore. It hurts too much and you don't know what she's capable of doing. I'll never be free of her, don't you understand?"

All she could think was that she needed to go back to not feeling anything and live alone again. She needed to rely only on herself and no one else. It's the only way people around her would ever be safe from Edna and her games. Kate learned new things every day and today she found out that she wasn't meant to be happy. It wasn't her destiny to have a man who loved her and friends. It wasn't in her cards.

If she stayed in Canon City, Jay's life would be turned upside down worse than it already was and he'd never forgive her. The knife in her heart told her it needed to end, she hated that thought, but she must leave. It was the only way out.

She could feel Jay's eyes on her. It would be difficult to leave him, but she knew she must. He couldn't be hurt by her stupidity. She loved him too much and he couldn't pay the price for her. She looked out the window and realized they were headed back to Jay's.

"Frank, please, take me to my apartment," she said between sobs.

"Kate, sweetheart, I'd rather have you stay at Jay's. You'll be safer there," Frank said over the seat.

"I don't fucking care if I'm safe. I want to get to my apartment." She looked out the window and continued to cry. She couldn't look at Jay; it would make her go insane.

"What did she say to you, Kate?" she heard Jay ask.

"It doesn't matter. I'm leaving."

"Fine, then I'll go with you," he said. "Frank, can we go back to your office? I'll need to pick up the Jeep."

Frank turned the car into a strip-mall lot and parked. He shut the car off and turned around in his seat. "What did she say, Kate?" he asked.

"I'm sorry I wasted your time, Frank." She leaned against the door and rocked back and forth. "You're a very good attorney, but she's too much and I don't think you know enough to fight her. In the long run, she will win if I don't get out of here."

"Kate, you didn't waste my time. Remember when I said she'd pushed your buttons for too long? You are letting her do it again. What did she say?"

"I told you before, it doesn't matter."

"It sure as hell must have mattered; you were white as a sheet when you came out of the conference room. Should I see if I can figure it out?" Frank's voice went deep and very serious.

She looked at him. "Please, let me out of the car."

"No, Frank. Don't let her out. She started to run in front of a truck," Jay said and reached for her.

She backed into the door away from him and felt tears continue to roll down her cheeks. "I promise not to run into the traffic, Frank. Please." She sounded flat even to herself. Between the sobs and sniffles, her promise didn't sound valid. She couldn't let herself feel anything or she'd come apart and would need a crazy house.

She heard a door open and glanced toward the front of the car. Frank got out, shut the door and leaned against it.

"You promised you wouldn't push me away, but since that wasn't true, how can I trust you not to hurt yourself?" Jay asked.

Kate heard the question, but only shrugged. "It was only a spur of the moment thing. I wouldn't have really done it. I don't want to be road kill." She couldn't look at him, it already hurt too much. If she looked into his beautiful brown eyes she'd break down and didn't think she'd ever stop crying. She realized her plan was dead in the water.

"Kate."

She heard pain in Jay's voice and felt his hand on her leg. She tried to get closer to the door, but there wasn't any more room. She wanted to fall into his arms and feel his strength and warmth, but knew she couldn't. It would give him the wrong idea and she didn't want that.

"I'm sorry if I've hurt you, Jay. It has to be this way."

Jay put his fingers under her chin and tried to turn her to face him, but she looked back out the window. "If you're going to break up with me, then you'll need to look me in the eye and tell me. It's the only way I'll believe you."

She felt her lip tremble and closed her eyes. She put her forehead on the window and felt the cool from the glass on her skin. "I can't...I don't know...it's too much."

"I don't know what your mom said to you, but we can get through..."

"No, *we* can't!" she shouted at him. "I have to leave."

"Okay then, as I said, I'll go with you. Where are we going? I want to call my folks so they don't worry and I'll need to make arrangements at the rink."

"No, you have to stay. The rink needs you, the hockey team needs you..." She started to cry all over again.

"Sweetheart, you need me worse than they do, right now. If it means we go for a while, then we'll do it."

Kate finally looked at him through the blur of tears. She wanted to agree with him, but knew she couldn't. It wasn't fair to him to take him away from his life. She looked at the back of the seats in front of her. "No, I don't want you to come with me and I don't need you." She looked back out the window.

His hand came up to her chin and turned her face. He moved his hand up her cheek and touched the tears. "Kate, look me in the eye and tell me that. Tell me you don't love me and the life we can have together is just a joke. Tell me to my face," he said, quietly.

She felt her eyes well up again and tried to look away, but he wouldn't let her turn her head. She couldn't say it, because she knew it would be a lie.

"I thought so. Did your mother threaten me?"

Kate felt the waterworks start all over again and run down her cheeks around his fingers. "Jay, I won't let her hurt you...I can't...I won't let it happen." Her voice faded and she put her hands over her face. "I don't understand how anyone can be this way."

"Babe," Jay whispered and pulled her over the seat into his arms. "Thank you for trying to protect me."

She tried to push away from him, but his arms wrapped around her. The idea of being safe didn't exist for her, even though Jay's hold on her should make her feel that way. She knew what damage a gossip mill could do and felt so afraid for Jay. She thought about that bitch, Monica, and didn't know what to do about that scenario. She heard the car door open and saw Frank get in and lean over the seat.

"You two are hugging, this is good. What did your mother say, Kate?"

"She threatened to do something to me," she heard Jay answer for her.

Kate kept her eyes closed and tried to stop crying. The front of Jay's sweatshirt was wet and she was pretty sure she looked horrible.

"What did she threaten?" Frank asked.

"She won't say, Frank," Jay said.

"Jay, could you get out of the car for a minute?"

"What? Why?"

"I need to talk to my client for a moment," Frank said. She could hear a stern attorney sound in his voice.

Jay huffed and started to loosen his grip on Kate. She looked up at him and knew she should say something, but couldn't figure out the right words to use.

"Are you okay, sweetheart?" Jay put his hand back onto her cheek.

"Yeah." She watched him open the door and unfold his tall frame from the seat. He slammed the car door and leaned against it. She looked over the seat at Frank, who handed her a couple of napkins.

"Those are from my non-existent lunch." He waited while she blew her nose and dried her cheeks. "Okay, Kate, its brass tacks time. What did she say?"

Kate looked at her hands and felt the fear overwhelm her. "She threatened Jay. She's been in touch with that Monica woman, who's going to say Jay raped her. Edna also said she would start a rumor that Jay is abusing some of the boys on the hockey team. Frank, it will ruin him and he'll never be able to have a serious business again. I know what rumors can do and it's not good. So you see...it's best, for Jay...I should leave and then Edna won't mess up his life."

She saw Frank get angry and then he nodded. "I'm going to start the suit, this afternoon. I think we can get these other threats under control, too." He looked at Kate. "Sweetheart, I don't want you to worry. I know you will, but let Jay take care of you. Try to relax and I'll be in touch this afternoon. Knock on that window and let lover boy know he can get back in."

Jay got back into the car and looked at them both. "So, did you tell him?"

Kate nodded. "Frank," her voice came out weak. "Let's go back to your office. Jay needs to pick up his Jeep." She wiped her eyes again with the napkins and held them tight in her hand.

"Frank's taxi service is happy to take you anywhere," he said as he pulled the car out of the parking lot.

"What are we going to do?" Jay asked.

"You two are going home and not making any moves until you hear from me later. I've got a couple of leaks in the dam to repair. I want you to relax tonight and try to get some rest. I know it will be hard, but just try."

Kate shrugged again and thought it didn't really matter. She needed to leave and let Jay get on with his life.

Chapter Twenty

When they got back to Jay's house, Kate washed her face and lay down on top of the comforter on his bed. Jay talked on the phone with the rink and she didn't want to know what arrangements he made. She needed to separate herself from him. As much as she hated it, she knew this was for the best. She put her hand over her eyes and took in a couple of deep breaths to keep from crying. As much as she didn't want to feel, she was miserable. Jay was such a good man and didn't deserve the unhappiness she'd brought into his life. She knew she needed to get away from him and leave Canon City. There wasn't anything else for her to do.

"Hey, sweetheart. Are you hungry?" he said.

She felt his hand on her hip. "No, I'm fine," she answered and rolled onto her side with her back to him.

He lay down behind her and put his arm around her. "No, you're not fine. I can tell by the tone of your voice and you're shaking again."

"I'm just tired of all of this. I thought for five minutes...never mind, it doesn't matter." She moved away from him and sat on the edge of the bed and then stood up. "I'm going outside."

"Can I come with you?" He rolled over and stood up.

"It's your house, Jay. You can do whatever you want." She went down the stairs and he followed her. At the double doors, she undid the lock and stepped onto the deck. She sat on the top step and looked out at the yard. There were tall trees and bushes all around the lawn. They looked wild and Kate wanted to be that free. Jay sat down next to her.

"You're not going to tell me what your mom threatened, are you?" He nudged her shoulder.

"Frank's going to take care of it. He said not to worry." She put her arms around her knees and put her head down.

"He's a really good attorney. I never would have thought he'd do so well when we were in high school. Frank never acted serious about anything then. I think his dad wanted him to be on the football team, but he did everything he could to do the opposite of what his dad wanted. He got really serious in college. When he went to law school his dad was pissed. His dad is a doctor and he wanted Frank to follow in his footsteps."

Kate felt his warm hand on the back of her neck. He rubbed it and her shoulders and back. It felt good and relaxing, but she didn't want that right now. She needed to stay alert, in case her mother tried to do something. Kate thought the restraining order was probably a joke. Her mother would do what she wanted. She pushed his hand away from her shoulder, but didn't move. She needed to make him not want her. How could she make him not want her, when all she wanted to do was fall into his arms? The plan snuck back into her brain and she thought she might be able to make it work.

"Hey, are you in there? You're so quiet," Jay asked near her ear. "I think I've asked you that already once today. Talk to me, Kate."

"Yeah, I'm in here. I just don't have much to say."

"Kate, you are scaring the crap out of me. I don't know what I can do to help you and it's making me feel like an idiot boyfriend. I know you're thinking about ways to get away from me and leave Canon City. If you want to continue to run, I can't stop you, but you can be damn sure I'm going to fight you tooth and nail, to get you to stay. I love you so much Kate, it's a wonder how I ever existed before we met." His voice began to crack and Kate turned her head to look at him. She could see tears in his eyes and it killed her to cause him such pain. "I want to trust that you're not going to try to leave, but I'm sorry, I can't and it's driving me nuts."

She sat up and put her arms around his ribs. The tears started to roll again. "I'm sorry I brought all of this into your life. Earlier, I tried to make you not want to be around me. I thought I could get you to want me to leave." She laughed and looked up at him. He was a blur through her tears. "That didn't work very well. I want you to hold me worse than anything. I don't want you to hate me."

"Oh babe, that's not going to happen." He wrapped his arms around her and pulled her tight to his chest. "I know we can make it through this. We just need to stay together and fight that bitch."

They held each other close for several minutes. Kate saw a movement out of the corner of her eye and jumped. She looked out at his yard and saw a deer stroll onto the lawn. It nibbled as it went along.

"Jay, look at that," she whispered.

They both watched the light brown deer walk around the yard. Kate thought it was the most beautiful thing she'd seen in a while. She leaned on Jay and felt amazed at the grace of the animal as it moved around the green grass. It slowly walked through some bushes and disappeared.

"That was the sweetest thing. I wish it were some sort of good luck sign, but I know that's not reality. I'm so angry with myself," Kate said.

"Why, sweetheart?" Jay looked down at her and put his fingers in her hair.

"I went into that meeting and when Frank gave all that information I didn't pay any attention. I just knew I didn't want to be there and two seconds later I felt scared again. I just knew I needed to get away from all that crap."

"You know, Frank said it a couple of days ago. Your mother brought you up that way. She trained you to be afraid of her and that's not something you're going to get rid of overnight. We'll get it worked out and if we need some professional help, we'll get it."

Kate put her head on his chest and closed her eyes. "I'm so tired."

"How about we have some of my mom's chicken casserole, and then crawl into bed. We'll just snuggle and sleep."

Kate looked up at him and touched his lips. "How did I get so lucky?" She stretched up to kiss him.

"See, you didn't think you deserved to be happy, but here I am." He kissed her nose.

"Here you are," she whispered. She closed her eyes as his lips came down. He gave her a gentle kiss. When she opened her eyes, he smiled down at her.

"I wish you'd tell me what the threat was," he said.

"Frank said he's going to take care of it. He looked really angry and it made me believe him."

Jay warmed up the casserole and Kate ate a little, but just wanted to sleep. She wanted everything from her past to disappear like the deer and let her rest for just a little while.

After they'd cleaned everything up in the kitchen, Jay scooped her off her feet and carried her up to the bedroom. She brushed her teeth and heard Jay's cell phone ring.

"Hey Frank, what's up?" She heard Jay answer. "What now?"

Kate dried her hands off, stood in the bathroom doorway and looked at Jay's back. He shook his head and put his hand on his hip.

"Kate's pretty wiped out. Can't this wait until tomorrow?" He turned around and looked at her. He crossed his eyes. "Frank, it's after nine o'clock." He put the phone to his chest. "Frank wants us to meet him at the rink. He says it's very important. Do you feel up to it, sweetheart?"

"I guess so. I'm glad I brushed my teeth." She grabbed her sneakers and sat on the end of the bed to put them back on.

"This better be good, Frank." He turned the phone off.

Kate felt his hand on her back and looked up at him. "It's okay, babe. Hopefully, it won't take long and then we can come back and sleep." She tried to smile.

"I'm sorry." Jay leaned over and kissed her. Turning around, he grabbed his own shoes and sat down next to her.

Kate put her hand on his arm. "Jay," she said softly. "You have no reason to apologize. This is all Frank's doing, not yours. We can blame him."

He laughed. "I know. I'll have to be sure to run him down at the next Broom Ball match." He stood up and offered his hand.

Chapter Twenty-One

When they walked through the front doors of the rink, Kate could hear voices and saw people sat up on the bleachers. Frank walked up to them and rubbed his hands together.

"Great, everyone is here. Let me explain where we're at," Frank said and looked straight at Kate. "These are all the parents of Jay's hockey team."

"Why are they here?" Jay interrupted and looked at the mass of people.

"Hush up and you'll find out. I've explained a little to them why we wanted them to come out tonight. I need for you, Kate, to tell them your story. Tell them about your mom, the threats, everything."

"What?" Kate took a step back and a knot landed in her stomach.

"Honey, you can do this. I know you're not used to speaking in front of people, but you did used to skate in front of an audience. They need to hear what happened, what your mom threatened and you need to remember who you're doing this for and why you're doing it. This is all for Jay and you, right? I know you can do this."

Kate felt her heart race and she became warm. She looked up at Jay.

"I won't leave your side, babe, I swear it. What the hell is this all about?" He took her hand and held on tight.

"Jay, you will find out. The other thing you need to know is that I've got the Canon City sheriff's department out looking for Monica and Sheriff Bennett is aware of the threat from her." He turned around and walked to the boards, in front of the crowd of parents. "Hey everyone, can I have your attention, please?" Frank said and held up his hands. The folks in the bleachers quieted down. "Thank you all for coming out with such short notice, but I need your help, as does Jay and his girlfriend, Kate Beck." Frank looked at them and waved them over.

Kate looked at the people who sat on the bleachers. She recognized some of the parents from the Saturday games.

"Kate will explain to you what's going on and why we need your assistance." He looked at her and nodded.

All of the parents looked at her, too. Her mouth went dry and she tried to swallow. She cleared her throat and put her hand on Jay's arm.

"Uh, okay," she started in a small voice. "I know some of you as Kate Beck, which is my legal name now, but I once went by the name Stacy Douglas. I was a figure skater and...well, all that's not really important." She looked up at Jay and focused on him. "I have a pretty weird mother, the ultimate bad sports parent. She's always gotten her way and when she doesn't get what she wants she can be really mean. She wants me to go back to California with her, but I want to stay here in Canon City and she threatened to do her terrible worst to make my life miserable if I do stay here." She looked back at the people and found faces she knew. "Everyone here is so kind and accepted me without many questions. I just don't want to leave. She's threatened Jay." She felt his hand tighten on hers. "She said she'd start a rumor that he is abusing the kids on his hockey team...really, bad stuff. She also might pay Monica Everett to say he'd raped her, and..." Kate's eyes started to cloud over. "It's not true, none of it. You guys know Jay. You have to know..."

"Kate." One of the dads stood and looked down at her. "I've already heard the rumor and know it's a load of horseshit. A lot of us grew up and went to school with Jay and we do know him. There's no way he'd ever do crap like that."

"Who did you hear it from, Dave?" Frank asked.

"It was some jerk with two black eyes and a Band-Aid over his nose."

Kate felt relieved to see several heads nod in agreement. Then one of the moms stood up.

"As for Monica Everett, I've felt for years that she ought to be run out of town. Your mother doesn't know what she's dealing with and, knowing Monica, she'll probably end up screwing your mom, one way or another." The woman sat down and crossed her arms.

Jay put his hands on her waist and pulled her back. Kate smiled. "Jay is very lucky to have such good friends."

"We keep telling him that, but he still won't give us free ice time," another lady said. There were several chuckles around her.

"Ok, free ice time this Sunday at two in the morning," Jay said, which caused the crowd to laugh again.

There were some groans and then another mom stood up. "Since we know what to expect, is there anything we can do to head your mom off? How can we help?"

"That's a great offer, but you don't need to get yourselves in trouble, too," Frank said. "I'd like to ask that you all keep me in the loop. If you hear anything, call my office and ask for my assistant, Jarod. He's up to date and any little thing we can put into a harassment suit will be accepted."

The parents started to file out and as they walked past Kate and Jay they shook hands and thanked them for the support. Kate saw some of the parent wore confidence in Jay on their faces, but there were a couple who may have felt some doubts. They didn't look convinced and she felt certain Jay might still be hurt in the long run.

When everyone except Frank was gone, the room seemed quiet. He sat on the bottom bleacher and rubbed his eyes. "Well, that went very smoothly, as I knew it would," he said.

Jay turned Kate around, held her tight and kissed her forehead. She felt so tired, but a flame started in her belly and moved into her legs.

"Frank, did you know my girlfriend is my hero?" Jay said and looked down at Kate. She leaned back and looked up at him. "That's right, babe. You protected me from your evil mother and I love it," Jay covered her lips with his.

"Oh dear, if you two are going to smooch, then I'm outta here." Frank stood up.

Jay looked over Kate's shoulder and she turned slightly. "Good night, Frank," Jay said.

Frank shook his head and grabbed his coat. "We'll talk tomorrow. Just remember, the front door's unlocked."

Kate turned back to Jay. She put her hand up on his cheek and looked into his beautiful brown eyes. "You know, this is the first time I've ever seen a group of people I barely know be so supportive. It's an amazing thing and I actually think everything is going to be fine." She moved up on her toes and kissed him.

"You need to remember lesson number one, sweetheart. The things I care for are protected by my family and friends. I know it takes some getting used to, but I think you can handle it, now."

She put her lips back on his and whispered, "Let's get out of here."

Chapter Twenty-Two

Kate felt bad that she'd lied to Jay. She didn't think everything was going to be fine. She knew how her mother worked. Anything could be possible and, as much as it killed her, she needed to walk away from Canon City and Jay. She didn't want anyone threatened or hurt anymore.

When they got back to Jay's house he'd wanted to take a quick shower and while he did that, Kate searched around his place for a piece of paper and wrote him a note. It read:

Dear Jay, I want you to know I do love you very much. You are a very gentle and patient man and I couldn't have hoped for more. I can't stay, though and watch my mother try to destroy you and all you've built here in Canon City. I can't stand the thought that I brought all of this down on you and can't find the strength to fight her. I will always love you and hope you can understand and forgive me. Kate

She folded the note and put it into the back pocket of her jeans that sat in a pile on the floor. The shower shut off and she jumped back under the covers on the bed. When Jay came out of the bathroom, he asked her why she wasn't asleep and she slid the covers down to expose her breasts.

"It seems I found just a small amount of energy left and have done nothing but lay here and wish you would come out of the shower to warm me up." She smiled.

Jay walked up to the bed and pulled the rest of the covers off her and admired her body. "Baby, you are so gorgeous." He leaned over and kissed the scar on her ribs and then put his lips on her nipple.

They made love and Kate did her best to wear him out. She teased his penis with her lips and channel and when he finally flipped her over on her back, he pumped her endlessly. She wanted him to be dead asleep soon. He came and his eyes crossed as he sucked in breath after breath. When Jay rolled off her, his eyes closed and he sighed.

"Babe, that was incredible. I'll have to remember how good you are at teasing fore-play," he said as his breaths evened out. After a bit, she heard him breathe very deep and he started to snore a little.

Kate wanted to fall asleep, too, but knew she must get up and leave. It was now or never. She quietly got up, grabbed her clothes off the dresser and got dressed in the living room. She left the note on the kitchen counter by the coffee maker and slipped out of the house.

The road stretched ten miles back to her apartment. She half ran and half walked it and tried to keep her lungs from the burn of over-exertion. Very few cars passed her and she tried to stay near street lamps, but in some places it turned very dark. The weather had also grown cold and she wished her coat was just a little bit thicker. It took her almost three hours, but eventually her apartment door came into view and she looked at her watch. It was four-fifteen in the morning.

She felt exhausted from the ten mile walk-run from Jay's, but she needed to keep moving. She looked at the bus schedule. It ran every hour from Canon City to Pueblo and when she looked at her watch, found she had about forty-five minutes to get packed and to the bus stop. She'd get to Pueblo and walk to the train station and take the first one out. She wasn't sure if she wanted to head north or south. That decision would be determined by the train schedule, but the first one to leave she'd be on. She'd shut her emotions off and would deal with them after she was on a train out of Colorado.

She grabbed the box that held her skates and the snow boots from the floor of the closet and stuffed them into the bag. She'd packed this thing so many times she didn't even need to think about it.

After she got all of her clothes put in, she grabbed a smaller bag and went into the bathroom to get her toiletries together. She picked up small bottles of shampoo and lotion, her toothbrush and make-up and put them into the small bag. She heard a noise behind her and as she turned, a hand with a white cloth came up over her face and another grabbed the back of her head.

Kate dropped the bag she held as everything around her went black.

****

Boone, the man hired by Max Hardy for his wife Edna, held the cloth over Kate's nose and as she started to fold up, moved his hand down her back to keep her from crumpling onto the floor. He adjusted his arms and put his free hand under knees to lift her up.

In the bathroom light, he looked down at her and found her to be very attractive. Boone smiled and thought, *Maybe I'll push the old woman out onto the highway and keep this one for myself.* He chuckled as he carried her out into the living room.

His partner, Troy, stood at the front door and kept watch.

"That went easier than I thought it would." He waited for Troy to swing the door open and then walked out to the driveway.

"Sneaky bastard. I didn't hear you at all," Troy whispered and moved ahead of him to open the back door of the SUV.

Mrs. Hardy looked at them from the front seat. Boone thought she looked like some weird primate that would pee its pants, she appeared so excited.

He carefully maneuvered Kate onto the seat and strapped the seat belt around her waist. He pulled a pair of hand cuffs out of his pocket and attached one to her wrist. He then put the other through the handle that hung above the door and pulled her other wrist up. After he'd gotten the cuffs secure, he slammed the door shut and walked to the other side of the vehicle and got in. As he pulled a blind fold out of his pocket and as he put it over Kate's eyes, he glanced at the woman in the front seat.

"Mrs. Hardy, she's going to start coming around in about fifteen minutes. I recommend you keep your trap shut. We need to get back to Denver without any problems. Once she's on the plane, you can do whatever you want." The woman, who sat on the front seat, had a shocked look on her face and turned to the front really quickly.

Boone smirked and secretly enjoyed the fact he'd offended the woman. She acted like such a snob.

****

Jay could hear his phone buzz and opened his eyes. He first wondered why Kate wasn't next to him and then sat up.

"Kate," he said and heard only silence. He switched the lamp on and picked up his phone. He saw Frank's name on the screen.

"What?" he said into the phone and headed for the stairs. He hoped Kate was out on the back deck. She seemed to like doing that and he knew she'd found it difficult to sleep the last few nights.

"Jay, I just got a weird call from Sheriff Bennett," he heard Frank say.

Jay stopped half-way down the stairs and waited.

"He said the woman that owns the house where Kate lives called in to report that a big man carried Kate out of the apartment. He put her into a black SUV and it took off."

Jay turned around and went back up the stairs.

"Bennett's over there now with his people and I'm on my way. He said it looks like someone broke in. They took the deadbolt out of the door and forced the doorknob lock."

Jay grabbed his pants and sat down on the end of the bed. He wedged the phone between his ear and shoulder and then leaned over to put his pants on. Before he stood up, he put on socks and his sneakers and then stood up pulling on his pants.

"Jay, do you have any idea what she was doing over there this early in the morning?"

"No Frank." He continued to move and pulled a sweatshirt out of a drawer. He turned and headed back for the stairs. "When we went to bed last night, everything seemed fine. Kate said she wasn't worried that much and seemed relaxed." He stopped at the top of the stairs. "Damn, I should have seen it." He went the rest of the way down the steps and turned into the hallway. "She said the way you handled the parents at the rink had given her confidence that everything would turn out fine. God, I'm such an idiot." He found his coat hanging on the closet doorknob and dug his keys out of the pocket. "I'm on my way Frank. I'll be there in five to ten minutes." He slammed the front door and headed for his Jeep. "Frank, I gave Kate a cell phone with GPS, just in case her mom decided to pull some weird shit."

"Do you have the number?"

Jay gave him the number and then threw his phone on the seat. He slipped the sweatshirt on and pulled his coat on over it. When he got the Jeep moving he tried not to speed, but ran three red lights.

The question *what was Kate doing?* kept running through his brain and he felt very confused. What happened since last night that caused her to go to her apartment in the middle of the night, alone? It hit him then that she would have been on foot.

He turned off the highway and followed her street. Up ahead he saw the police cars with their lights on and Frank's car. He pulled behind the BMW and as soon as the Jeep was shut off he jumped out and ran down the driveway. He walked through the open doorway and Frank and the sheriff both looked at him. Frank nodded and walked toward him. Jay wanted to know what was being done right now to find Kate. He started to feel panicked and didn't like it. Frank put his hand on Jay's arm.

"Mrs. Davenport, upstairs, said that Kate looked asleep when she was taken out of here. The black SUV sounds like the same one that we saw the day you plugged one of those guys. The one her mother rode in. Sheriff Bennett's got the electronic specialists in Pueblo searching for the GPS on Kate's phone. I just hope she has it turned on." Frank stopped and looked around. "Jay, I've got to ask. Is there any possibility that Kate just went with them?"

Jay looked at his friend and wanted to hit him in the face. "No, no way. She wanted nothing to do with that woman."

Frank nodded. "Good, I agree. The State Police want to put this off for two days. If they get her out of the state, things could get really difficult."

"Frank, she wouldn't just go..."

"I know, Jay. Don't worry, we'll get her back. The highway patrol from here to Denver and all the way south to Colorado Springs is on alert." The sheriff called out Frank's name. "Stay here. I'll be right back."

Jay watched him walk over to the sheriff. He felt as though he were in a dream and never in his life felt so helpless. He wanted to save Kate and then wanted her to explain clearly, with no lies, what she'd been thinking about when she'd left his house in the middle of the fucking night. He put a hand in his hair and walked toward the bedroom. He looked at the bed and remembered that wonderful first time they'd made love. He'd known on that day, deep in his heart, that he wanted her with him, always. Then he saw the duffle bag and realized what she'd been doing. She'd planned to leave him and Canon City behind. He wanted to hit something so bad he turned around and started back for the front door. He needed air.

Frank caught up with him outside. "The highway patrol has caught up with them. They're about an hour and half south of Denver. There's a private air field out there and that's where they seem to be headed. We might as well have a seat. We won't hear anything for a bit."

Jay looked at his friend. "I'm going to stay out here for a few minutes. I need the air."

Chapter Twenty-Three

Kate could hear men's voices every now and then as she started to come around. She thought she'd been hit with a sledgehammer and already felt a nasty headache bang at her temples. Her arms hurt and her hands were asleep.

It took a few minutes before she realized she couldn't open her eyes. Something covered them and felt tied very tightly at the back of her head. It pulled at her hair. She could feel motion and knew she rode in a car.

Her first thoughts were that her mother finally succeeded in getting what she wanted. It wasn't a fact, but Kate felt it deep in her heart that her mother caused this latest development. The voice in her head started to whine that if she'd just stayed in bed with Jay, this wouldn't have happened. She tried to shift in the seat to get some sensation back into her hands.

"Good morning, sweetheart," she heard a low gravelly voice whisper and fingers brushed against her cheek. She flinched back and hit the window with her head. She tried to move her hands and discovered her wrists were tied or cuffed to the handle above the door. She felt the stranger's fingers move her coat and run along the side of her breast.

Kate squirmed and with both hands grabbed the handle and brought her leg up. She kicked out and hit something, but a pair of hands grabbed onto her leg and held it tight. A man laughed and put his hand on her thigh.

"My, my, aren't you a little tiger?" He latched onto her leg and started to move his hand up the inside of her thigh.

Kate felt awake enough to keep her wits about her, even though she still had a headache. She brought her other leg up fast and kicked out. She didn't know what she hit, but the next thing she knew she got punched in the jaw by a hard fist.

"Bitch, do you want me to knock you out again?"

"If you're going to rape me you might as well try. I will fight you, asshole," she hissed.

"Boone, knock it off. Max won't be happy if she's all bruised up. When we get back to Los Angeles, she'll have some work to do right away."

"Fuck, Max. I think I deserve a little taste of her and she has great breasts. I want to see her naked from head to toe."

Kate heard her mother's voice. She now knew for certain this was Edna's work. She wanted to scream at that deranged woman and scratch her eyes out, pull her hair and bruise her soul the way Kate felt she'd been bruised over the years. She was at a complete loss of what to expect and hated her mother more than ever. She would have started to cry, but couldn't find the tears.

"Boone, I do fuck Max. If you're going to screw my daughter, then chloroform her again to keep her from screaming, I'd rather not hear it, and don't hit her anymore."

Kate couldn't believe her ears. Her mother was insane and she thought about starting to scream if that man came near her. As she wished to be knocked out again so she wouldn't have to face any kind of abuse.

"Hey, we got a problem," a new voice piped up.

"What?" the one called Boone said.

"There are two or three cops behind us with their lights on. Asshole, did you check her pockets?"

She felt the stranger's hands move around her jacket and when he slid one into her outside pocket, he pulled out her cell phone. She thought to leave it behind at Jay's but forgot in her hurry to leave. Kate felt relieved until she felt something sharp stab into her leg and she began to feel fuzzy again.

****

Sheriff Bennett walked into Kate's apartment. He held his phone up to his ear. Jay paced back and forth in the kitchen, while Frank sat at the table going through some papers.

The sheriff turned off his phone and came all the way into the kitchen. "The highway patrol got them on I-25. They tried to pretend Kate was asleep, but since the patrol was alerted to her likeness, they didn't have a problem identifying her. The kidnappers apparently knocked her out with something. She's being taken to Parkview Hospital in Pueblo just until she wakes up and they make sure she's okay."

Jay bolted out the door and up the driveway to his Jeep. He sat for a moment in the seat and looked at his cell phone. He tried to remember why he looked at it, but all he could think of was Kate. He knew from the bag on her bed that she'd planned to leave him, and wished he could have gotten through to her that she would be safe if she stayed with him. Somewhere along the lines, she'd freaked and felt she couldn't turn to him for help.

He keyed in Parkview Hospital in Pueblo to get directions and when it came up, he reached forward to start the engine on his vehicle. He wanted her to tell him why she'd tried to run.

Chapter Twenty-Four

Kate couldn't hear anything for the longest time. Not that she'd gone deaf, but wherever she'd been taken, there wasn't any noise at all. The quiet scared her. She remembered she heard voices that sounded very far away and they seemed to talk about her, but otherwise it was quiet and she thought it should be peaceful. She knew that man and her mother must be somewhere near her and tried to get her head clear enough to come up with a plan - not that her plans tended to work. The last one fell apart and crumbled to dust.

When she tried to open her eyes she couldn't keep them open. She didn't know how long she lay there flat on her back, but one thing she knew for certain, she needed to roll over. Her lower back felt like it was bound in a vise.

As she tried to turn, she felt a hand on her arm and it became apparent that the hand attempted to help her roll over, but the memory of what that hand did to her crashed back into her head. She swung her arm out and tried to push the hand away. She fought as best she could but felt exhausted and finally stopped. She could hear Jay's voice and prayed she wasn't hallucinating or in a dream.

The hand continued to hold hers tightly and she opened her eyes. She saw Jay look down at her and it wasn't the friendly face she remembered. He looked angry and his beautiful brown eyes were pinched. His brow folded down.

"Please, let go of my hand, Jay," she croaked.

"Where are we going?" he asked.

"I don't know where you're going, but I have a bus to catch." She brought her hand up and saw an IV in her arm. "Where am I?" she whispered.

"Frank's on his way. He wants to talk to you. He's pretty pissed, too."

"No. There's nothing to talk about. Jay, the longer I stay the more you'll be hurt and I can't take it. If you'd just read the note I left you'd understand. Please, just let me go," Kate said and tried not to let her voice rise. She thought maybe she'd finally made him mad enough at her, that he realized she wasn't worth wasting his time.

Kate saw Frank walk in the door with a cup of coffee in his hand. "Kate, you're awake. How do you feel?"

"I have a headache. Where is this place?" She frowned at Jay and began to push herself into a sitting position. "Would you, please, let go of my hand?" she barked at Jay.

"You're in Parkview Hospital. We have some things to discuss, my dear," Frank said and grabbed a straight back chair. He put it next to her bed and sat down.

"There is nothing to talk about. I appreciate everything you guys have done for me, but..."

"No buts, Kate." Frank put his hand on her arm. "Jay, let her go."

Jay looked down at her and Kate knew at that moment he was done. She hated that she'd made him so angry, but it would be for the best. She needed to leave and then he could look for a good woman to make him happy. He released her hand and that one action just about broke her heart for good. She looked away from him and bit her lip to keep it from trembling.

"Sweetie, just hear me out, please," Frank said.

Kate looked at the clock on the wall. "I've missed the bus, so you have a little time."

"Good. Jay, would you wait out in the hallway a minute? I need..."

"You need to speak to your client alone. We've been there. Whatever." Jay stood up and left the room. "I'm out of here."

Kate heard the anger in his voice and instead of being afraid she just felt sad. She swore to herself, then and there, that she'd never get involved with anyone again. She felt guilt at what she'd done to him and never wanted to feel it again. She looked at Frank and waited for him to start his lecture. She felt pretty certain he would tear into her for trying to run.

"Kate, I can't keep you from running. I'd like to convince you to stay, but in the end, it's your decision. You're going to do what you want. My friend outside that door is not a very happy camper right now. My problem with you being my client and Jay as a friend makes this difficult. I'm perched on a fence and don't want to fall off." Frank crossed his arms over his chest and huffed. "First of all, we need to let the cops know if we're going to press charges against your mother and her stooges. The cops will wait patiently for only so long. I'll ask you now. Do you want to press charges?

"What happens if I do? Will I have to stay in Canon City and testify?"

"Unless your mother plea bargains and I don't see that happening, there will be a court case and, yes, you'll have to testify."

"I don't ever want to see her again, Frank. If I don't press charges then she'll go free and be a threat. I'll still have to run and hide, but at least Jay won't be ruined."

Frank nodded. "Something like that. I don't recommend it. Running will make you feel very alone. Kate, you have friends here and they care for you very much."

"I know, Frank. I've lived with being alone most of my life and know it very well, believe me."

"I do believe you, Kate." He shifted in his seat. "I have another idea and if it works, then it would keep your mother away from you for life. I've got a call into a circuit judge in Pueblo and I'll give you the full details after I'm sure we can proceed. I don't want to get your hopes up." Frank adjusted in his seat, again, and put his hand on her arm. "Sweetie, on another note, I think you know how Jay reacts when he's lied to. When you told him you thought everything was going to be fine last night, he took it at face value. I also know you're aware of the woman who lied to him about the baby. He's still not forgiven her and I can tell you, if you do stay, you may have lost him already."

"I don't want to put him through anymore, Frank. Jay deserves better than what I can give him. I must have been crazy to think I could have a real relationship. Sometimes things from the past keep coming back and..." She looked at him. "Never mind, it's not important. After that meeting with the parents at the rink last night, even though they know him, I could see in some of their faces they had doubts. I'm sure some of them went home and talked to their kids and asked questions. Jay's a good man and he loves those kids. He'd never do anything to harm them. I'm the one who brought this down on him and he doesn't deserve it."

"Kate, you are the best thing that's ever happened to that big idiot. I've never seen him act this way about anybody and I've known him a long time. I hate the thought that your mother is going to get away with all of this. I also hate that you're letting her. As long as you're in Canon City you are my client and I'll take care of you to the best of my abilities." He fisted his hand around hers and looked at her with a smile. "Kate, I know I'm being redundant, but please, don't let her win and make you go back to hiding. I know you're used to that lonely world, but there could be so much more for you if you just stand your ground against your mother. We can beat her. You know this and there are a lot of people who believe that, too; present company included."

"I know you and Jay care, but I'm really not worth it. I've never faced what went on with my mother back then and it scares me too much to even think about those days. It's always been easier to run. Jay deserves better than what I can give him, because I'm nothing, really." She put her hand in her hair and shook her head.

"You know, I've never in my life wanted to hit a woman, but I will, if you don't wake up and realize you are worth it. I think so and I'm sure if you hadn't lied to Jay, he'd feel that way, too. You are worth fighting for, but it's a two-way street, Kate. You have to want to help and fight for yourself." Frank stood up and turned away. He stomped through the door and then came back in. "Jay seems to have left. I'll find out how soon we can spring you from here and get you home."

Kate knew Jay was gone for good and he wouldn't come back. The look on his face appeared full of anger with her and she'd done the worst thing possible to him. The lie was there and no matter how hard she wished it the lie would never go away.

She put her hands over her face and felt the tears start from her eyes. She tried to remember when she'd last had a decent night's sleep. Everything around her seemed to slow down and speed up, but didn't give her the time to catch up.

She looked at the clock on the wall and realized it was seven-thirty in the evening, not the morning. Just several hours ago she and Jay made passionate love to the point of getting his sheets damp with sweat. She'd had everything she could possibly want in the world with him, but she'd thrown it away. She blinked and realized her actions brought her back around to the start.

"What goes around..." she whispered.

She was alone again, with no one to count on but herself. She kicked the covers off her legs and sat up on the side of the bed. Her head spun and she thought she should just go back to sleep and never wake up again. It would be the easiest. Then she'd never have to run from her mother again. She would just end.

*****

Jay walked into his house, shut the door and twisted the lock. He felt no desire to see or hear from anyone. He took his cell phone out of his pocket and threw it across the living room. It hit the glass doors that led to the deck. The throw shattered the phone and the glass in the wood frame.

He didn't know what to do next. He took his jacket off, dropped it onto the floor and walked into the kitchen. He opened a cupboard. The bottle of whiskey looked down at him. As he turned to lean on the counter, he saw a piece of paper on the counter by the coffee maker. He opened the fold and read Kate's note.

Dear Jay, I want you to know I do love you very much. You are a very gentle and patient man and I couldn't have hoped for more. I can't stay, though and watch my mother try to destroy you and all you've built here in Canon City. I can't stand the thought that I brought all of this down on you and can't find the strength to fight her. I will always love you and hope you can understand and forgive me. Kate

"Bullshit!" he shouted at the paper and crumpled it in his hand. He turned back around and took the whisky off the shelf and set it on the table. He breathed hard and felt pissed. He looked at the door on the cupboard and reached up, applied all his strength and pulled it off the unit. He swung it and knocked things off the counter. A salt shaker spun through the air and scattered salt around in circles before it crashed to the floor. He pulled dishes off the shelves and sent them flying, along with glasses and coffee mugs.

After he'd finished with the top shelves he started on the bottom and pulled out the drawers. He emptied them out, scattering the contents around the room and then stomped them to pieces. He kicked the debris around the room and then bellowed at the top of his lungs.

He looked around the kitchen, out of breath. "Women are fucked," he said between breaths. He grabbed the bottle of whisky off the table and walked into the living room where he flopped onto the couch. He kicked his shoes off and put his feet on the coffee table.

The remote control for the TV was wedged between the cushions on the couch. He put on some mindless sports program and turned the volume up loud. Unscrewing the lid off the bottle, he tipped it up and took a couple of hefty swallows. "I can't fucking get drunk fast enough," he mumbled.

Chapter Twenty-Five

One week later

      Libby Hager pulled her car into her son's driveway and parked. Every-other-week she made a visit to Jay's house to make sure he had some good food in his refrigerator. Her son tended to eat too much fast food and she wanted to be sure he got something healthful every now and then. She'd made a bucket of fried chicken and a couple of salads to get him through the week. One of the salads was potato and he insisted it was his favorite. She'd tried to call him this week, but his phone wasn't working or he'd turned it off. She hoped it meant he and Kate spent lots of quality time together.

      She parked next to Jay's Jeep and got out of her car. She slammed the door shut, grabbed two shopping bags out of the back and headed to the front door. When she found it locked, she set the bags down and got her keys back out of her purse. She could hear the TV through the door and wondered about that. Jay didn't watch much television.

She opened the door and picked up the bags. As she turned into the kitchen, she stopped dead in her tracks. The room was torn to pieces and Libby became concerned something very bad happened to her son.

"Jay!" she tried to shout over the loud TV.

She set the bags on the dinner table and went into the living room. She saw Jay's long body stretched out on the couch and three empty whiskey bottles on the coffee table. Jay wore a pair of jeans and that was about it. She moved to the TV and turned it off. Libby pulled her cell phone out of her jacket pocket and hit the speed dial.

"Hi honey," her husband answered.

"Mike, I'm at Jay's. I need you." She looked at her son's back as he began to move.

"What's wrong?"

"Just come now, Mike."

****

Jay felt the world move around him and it must have snowed. He sat in a very cold place and tried to open his eyes.

The next thing he knew something frozen stabbed at him and hit his body. His eyes shot open. He found himself in the bath tub with the shower spraying him with cold water. He tried to get up and saw his dad lean over and put a very strong hand on his chest.

"How long have you been drunk, Jay?" his dad asked.

Jay tried to look up at him, but the cold water splashed in his eyes. "What day is it?"

"Wednesday."

"I guess a week or so."

"What happened in the kitchen?"

Jay leaned over the side of the tub and could look at his dad. "What do you mean?"

"Your kitchen is torn to pieces. It looks like a cyclone blew through." His dad raised his eyebrows.

Jay sat back and began to get a little used to the cold water. "I got a little pissed off."

"A little?" His dad moved from the edge of the tub and sat on the toilet. "Jay, you're going to have to replace a lot of your stuff out there. I don't think your mom has found one dish that isn't broken."

"Mom's out there?" Jay sat up and started to stand.

"Are you sure you want to get out of the bath? Your mom is ready to lecture you pretty good on that mess. Maybe you need to sober up some more."

Jay laughed. "I haven't had anything to drink since last night. I'm just really hung over and have a flaming headache."

"I hope you've got some aspirin. Your mom is not very happy with you. Get cleaned up." His dad walked out and shut the door.

Jay took off his soaked jeans and under-drawers, and got the hot water going. He let the spray hit his face and hoped the headache would lighten up. He washed his hair and stopped for a second. It occurred to him that he couldn't remember how he got upstairs into the bath tub and then thought about his dad. The old man was stronger than Jay realized. He went back to his hair and started to think about Kate.

He rinsed his hair and leaned against the wall. He wondered where she was and if she'd left Canon City. He'd have to call Frank and find out what happened. He may be pissed off at her, but he still cared.

Jay went down the stairs and found his mom and dad swept up the mess. His dad carried a garbage bin out the door and his mom stood by the stove with a scowl on her face. They'd stacked pieces of drawer and cupboard along the back wall and his silverware sat on the counter in a shiny pile.

"Somehow you managed not to break the coffee pot." She scowled at him.

"Thank God. That would have meant the end of the world had happened." He tried to smile at her.

"It still may be the end of the world. You broke all of your coffee cups." She crossed her arms.

"Wait one second." Jay held up a finger and walked out of the kitchen. He went back up the stairs and collected mugs he'd left in the bedroom and his office. He carried them back down to the kitchen and bumped his mom away from the sink. He washed them quickly and then dried them. "Can I offer you a cup of coffee, Mom?"

"Smart ass." She took the full cup from him and pointed to the table.

Jay took his cup to the table and handed one to his dad as he came back into the room. He then sat down and looked up at his mom.

She peered into the oven and then turned back around. "The only thing not broken was a pie tin and your silverware. Thank you for not killing the refrigerator. Jay, what happened here?"

"I got a little pissed off."

His dad laughed. "He tried to tell me that one, too, honey. I'd say it maybe was a bit more than a little, my boy."

"Well," Jay looked at the kitchen. "I'd thought about remodeling the cabinets. I guess I have a good excuse now."

"Jay, I read the letter." His mom pulled Kate's letter out of her pocket. She'd smoothed it out as best she could. "Where's Kate? She said she lied to you."

"Yeah, she did." He looked into his coffee cup. "I don't know where she is."

"So you read this letter and let me guess, you started to compare her to Mandy Parker, the queen of lies?"

"Mom, you don't know the story..."

"I know enough about you, Jason Hager. I know how you get when someone lies to you. I've never understood where it came from, but let me tell you something. No one in this world is perfect and if you're going to be so unforgiving, you'll never find anyone to enjoy your life with."

Jay had never heard such forceful words come from his mother. He saw his dad reach over and put his hand over hers.

"Libs, maybe it's time we told him the truth," his dad said.

"No."

"Sweetheart, he's old enough and I think mature enough to know what happened."

"Oh God, you guys aren't going to tell me I'm adopted or something?" Jay sat up straight in his chair and felt truly concerned.

The lines around his dad's eyes crinkled. "Sorry to disappoint you, but you are ours, now and forever. No, Jay, I'm afraid I had a transgression once a long time ago."

His mom looked at him. "Mattie was just a baby and you were two years old."

"Jay, I had an affair..." his dad started.

"But he came clean with me. He told me the truth. It took a while, but we were able to work things out," his mom finished for his dad.

"The most important thing from that whole mess, was that your mother forgave me and we are better now than we were before I acted so stupid. I didn't think I would ever forgive myself for what I did to your mother. I betrayed her."

"That's right, Jay. Before you boys came along, we both were pretty selfish and we took a lot for granted. After that little bit of upset, things just got better and better."

"Mom, I appreciate the sentiment, but I'd already forgiven Kate once. How often will I have to keep that up?"

"In the letter she said she would give up everything with you so that you'd be safe. It must have broken Kate's heart to do that. I'd love to be able thank her for putting you first."

Jay sat back in his chair. "Mom, it's just not that easy for me. I don't want to go through what I felt with Mandy and...Kate's a great woman and if I ever get around to telling you her story, you'll be amazed at her strength, but I just can't..." Jay stood up and went to the coffee pot. "I need to think," he mumbled and closed his eyes. He'd never thought of what his mom just said. Kate put him first and tried to protect him.

"Jay, tell us her story now. Why did she think you weren't safe," his dad asked.

He turned from the counter and took in a heavy breath. He picked up the coffee pot and topped off their cups, then poured more into his mug. He didn't even know where to start, but sat down and related as best he could what happened to Kate and the arrival of her mother. He left out the part about how Edna wanted to take Kate back to Los Angeles to perform in porn movies. For that alone, Jay wanted to beat the woman to pieces. He just told his parents that Edna was a control freak and didn't like the fact the Kate could make it on her own for eight years.

When he stopped he looked around the table at his parents. His mother's eyes welled with tears and he almost joined her in a good cry.

"That woman should be shot," his mom said and dried her eyes. "How can any parent in their right mind...? Well, obviously that woman isn't in her right mind. Poor Kate must have been so frightened. Jay, we've got to help her and show her that there is some sanity in the world."

"Mom." He stood up. "I tried to protect her and keep her away from that bitch, but all Kate knows is how to run. I asked her to stay and she decided to do something else." He moved from the table and left the room.

****

Kate heard a car pull up in the driveway and a horn honk. She picked up her bag and went outside. She saw Frank wave at her from his BMW, locked the new dead bolt and walked to the car door.

After she'd belted in, Frank backed the car to the road and headed to the highway. They were on their way to Pueblo.

"Okay, Kate, here's what to expect. The judge will state the case as it stands now. Your mom and her cronies will be charged with kidnapping with the intent to take you across state lines to California. Are you with me so far?"

Kate nodded and said she understood what Frank told her.

"Then the judge is going to hit all of them with a healthy fine."

She saw Frank smile. "What is the fine for?" she asked.

"Well, primarily for the punch you took in the jaw, but, also, the lab tests that were done in the hospital showed you were given a date rape drug. There is no proof they had any malicious intent, but they're not going to get away with it." He smiled at her again. "The fine will be the topper. It's pretty high. They'll have to take the deal."

"What's the deal?"

"This is where things could get tricky. The judge will offer to freeze the charges and the fine, and they'll be banished from the State of Colorado. If they ever cross the state line in your lifetime, the charges will be unfrozen and they will be arrested. If they break that law and with the other charges, they could be put away for a very long time."

"Banishment? Is that even legal?" Kate felt stunned.

"It's not done a lot these days, but it is in the Constitution in a limited form and the case I quoted - Hamm v. Mississippi - was recent. It does stipulate that the defendants First, Fifth and Fourteenth

Amendment rights not be violated. If they choose to fight it - and they could, but it would be ridiculous, the court costs alone would be astronomical - then things could be difficult. The catch is, if they choose not to accept the deal that means we press on with the charges and there will be a court case. You would have to testify."

"What if I choose not to press charges?" She saw the look on Frank's face turn slightly angry.

"Sweetheart, you already know the answer to that one."

Kate looked out the front window. "Run and hide."

"Right, and unless you really enjoy that, I wouldn't recommend it."

They went silent for several miles. Kate thought it didn't really matter if she continued to run and hide. She didn't have anything that held her to Canon City. Not anymore. She could go back to being a ghost and no one would know the difference.

"Kate, have you heard anything from Jay?"

She felt her throat tighten and closed her eyes. "No."

"I've tried to call him, but his phone must be switched off. It's not even going to his voicemail. I may swing by his place this afternoon. Do you want to come with me?"

Kate looked at him. "No, I don't want to bother Jay."

"Kate..."

"Frank, drop it, please. I don't want to see him, okay?"

He glanced at her and huffed. "I know that isn't true, but I'll leave it alone for now."

She stared at her hands and wanted this over with. This day, she hoped, would be the last time she would see her mother.

Kate sat next to Frank in Judge Patrick Wilhelm's office. Two men sat on the other side of Frank with her mother and then the two men she'd hire to kidnap Kate sat alongside. One of the men was her mother's attorney, Mr. Levine. She found out later the other man was the attorney's assistant. A woman walked in with a stenotype machine on a small, round table. She went to a chair and sat down. She asked everyone in the room to give their full legal names and typed them into the machine.

It wasn't a court room. It appeared to be a simple office with a huge wooden desk and shelves and shelves of books. Kate wondered if the judge read all of those books and then focused her attention on the judge. He was an older man with gray hair and eagle eyes. He'd glance on occasion at the others in the room and when he looked at Kate, she froze in her seat. His looked softened though and she thought she didn't need to feel so nervous. He looked like a grandfather type. She watched as he flipped through the papers an assistant gave him and then he raised his head.

"Mr. Levine." The judge looked over his glasses.

Her mother's attorney stood up. "Yes."

"Have you had enough time to review this decision with your clients?"

"We have, Your Honor."

"And do your clients accept the stipulations set down in this agreement that they will not return to the State of Colorado in their lifetimes and will have no further contact with Miss Beck?"

Kate heard someone laugh and the attorney half-turned and frowned. "They do understand those terms, Your Honor."

The judge continued to look grimly over the top of his glasses. "Do your clients understand that should they return to Colorado the charges will be reinstated, as will the fine of five hundred-thousand dollars per offender? Do they understand that any appearance by them in this state will give Mr. Donnelly the opportunity to re-open the harassment lawsuit?"

"They do, Your Honor."

"Fine. Miss Beck," the judge said and looked at her.

She stood up and Frank moved up with her and put his arm over her shoulder. "Yes, sir."

"Do you understand the terms of this agreement as arranged by your consul, Mr. Donnelly?"

"I do, sir."

"Do you agree with these terms?"

"Yes, sir."

"Fine. Court reporter, do you have any questions?"

"No, sir," the woman at the small table said.

"Mr. Levine, your clients will be escorted to a flight from Denver International Airport to LAX where they will be released from custody. This session is finished. There is a notary next door who will witness the signatures to this agreement." He hit a gavel on his desk and several burly police officers entered the office. They escorted her mother, who refused to look at her, and the other two men out of the room. Kate didn't realize until then that all three were handcuffed. The two attorneys followed them out and the door shut behind them.

Kate looked up at Frank. "So, that's it?"

"That's it." He looked past her shoulder and smiled. "You'll just need to sign the agreement, but we'll wait a few minutes for the others to do it and leave the room so you won't have to see them."

Kate felt a hand on her elbow and was turned around. The judge stood in front of her. He took her hand and held it with both of his.

"Miss Beck, when Mr. Donnelly presented your case to me, I have to admit I felt very moved by your courage. I applaud you and wish you the very best." He winked at her.

"Thank you, sir." Kate felt shocked he'd spoken to her and didn't know how to react.

He shook hands with Frank. "Tell your dad I'll be up for golf next Sunday." He turned and went back to his desk.

Frank led her to the notary next door and after they signed the papers went down a hallway. They walked out of the courthouse into the noon-time sun.

"Do you want to go get some lunch and celebrate?" Frank asked and opened the car door for her.

"No, I have to work tonight. We'd better get back." Kate slid onto the seat.

Frank leaned on the door. "I could always call Harry to let him know you might be late."

She looked up at him and smiled. "I don't do late, Frank. Maybe we can celebrate another day." Kate put the seatbelt on and sat back.

Frank maneuvered the car onto the highway. "What about your dad, Kate? Are you ready to talk to him?"

She looked at Frank and almost started to cry. "He's really the only family I have left. I suppose that would be good."

"Can I tell Jay the good news?"

Kate bit her lip and then the water works started. She looked away from Frank and pretty much cried all the way back to Canon City.

Chapter Twenty-Six

Two weeks before Christmas 2014

Kate slept until late that afternoon and got up in time to go to work. She stayed in Canon City and decided to wait out the winter and move on in the spring. She called Frank and let him know she planned to stay for now.

Since Kate's mom decided not to fight the lawsuit and accepted banishment from Colorado, Frank felt there would be nothing further to worry about at this time. He confided to Kate that he felt very much that her mother needed mental health help. The fact that she'd given up so easily made him wonder if she wouldn't try something else in the future, but then laughed and said Kate would probably have five kids by then and be too out of shape to appear in any films. When Kate asked him who the supposed father of the five kids would be, he'd just smiled and tweaked her chin. He did say that now that Edna no longer existed, the time had come for her to live in the present and enjoy the fact that she didn't need to run anymore.

Frank set up a visit with Kate's father and in the second week of November, he arrived in Canon City. They'd met for lunch and talked until late in the evening. He explained a lot of what happened between him and her mom as Kate grew up. Her parent's relationship was stormy and her father felt extreme guilt at not being more attentive to the way things went for Kate. After he explained about her mother's infidelities, which he didn't know about until after Kate left for Colorado Springs, he apologized and told her that he should have stepped in more when Edna got on one of her rolls, but he never knew how to handle or control the woman. They spent a week talking off and on. Then he left to return to Portland. He invited Kate for Christmas, but she said she'd already been scheduled to work.

She'd told Harry she would be happy to work the week of Christmas and let the other wait staff be at home with their families. She'd told her father she would try to go to Portland in the spring. Maybe she would move back to her hometown.

She stayed away from the rink. She didn't want to get in Jay's way or make him think she stalked him. She missed keeping track of the young figure skaters when they practiced with their coaches and she missed the Saturday morning hockey matches. According to Frank, the Mighty Red Rockers were doing okay in the league. Jay turned over the main coaching duties to one of the assistants and very seldom showed up for the games. There weren't any Broom Ball games scheduled until after the New Year.

Mrs. Hager and Lark Stone turned up at the diner at least once a week. When she first saw Mrs. Hager after her case got settled, the woman gave Kate a hug that threatened to last a couple of minutes. When she pulled back, she saw tears in Mrs. Hager's eyes and wanted to know if she was all right. She told Kate that Jay explained some of the story to her and Mr. Hager and it broke her heart to think a parent could treat a child so poorly. She then insisted Kate learn how to cook and wouldn't take no for an answer. Kate would either ride the bus or walk out to the Hager's house and spend an afternoon learning the ins and outs of the culinary world. Mr. Hager became her test subject and never seemed to object to anything she made. Kate had a lot of fun and ended up buying a food processor.

They'd invited her for Thanksgiving, but Kate begged off. She knew that would be a family occasion and if Jay intended to be there, she didn't want to make him uncomfortable. She'd stayed home that night and half-ate a turkey TV dinner. The thing tasted wretched and she only ate a little before she tossed it into the trash.

One afternoon, Mrs. Hager asked Kate if she would help her serve at the Community Christmas Festival. Kate heard some noise about this at the diner, but asked Mrs. Hager what the evening was all about. She explained that just before Christmas, every year, the community came together for a night of good food, dancing and friendship. There would be several tables with salads, breads, and pasta dishes. A gentleman name Dave Taylor always manned a huge barbeque outside the center with ribs, burgers, and steaks. Some other women, a Mrs. Metcalfe and Mrs. Bickens always fought a dessert war with pies and cookies. Mrs. Hager was in charge of some salads and cake. They charged nominal prices for the food and all proceeds went to the Children's Auxiliary. She looked at Kate and said she knew she begged, but really needed the help.

When Kate broke down and agreed, she found out that on her next day off, Mrs. Hager and Lark were going to take her over to Pueblo to buy a dress for the party. While they shopped Kate asked Mrs. Hager if Jay would be at the festival. His mom wasn't sure. She said he usually attended, but he'd been in such a snit since their break up, that she just didn't know if he planned to come out or not.

After she tried on about fifteen dresses, Kate found one that looked acceptable to her and the other women. It was a black eyelet lace, fitted at the waist and belted. It came just above her knees but flared out a little. It also had straps on top and Kate found a pretty waist-length royal blue sweater to wear on top so she wouldn't freeze. The front dipped down and Lark said she'd need a good push-up bra to accentuate her cleavage. Kate blushed, but found herself in another dressing room and tried on a bra that she could barely breathe in.

They stopped for lunch and Lark told Kate how her husband, Charlie, proposed to her at last year's festival. He done it in front of the whole community and Kate thought it was the most romantic thing she'd ever heard. Charlie got up onto the stage with the DJ and used a microphone to surprise her.

After lunch, when Kate stopped to pick up a pair of pantyhose, Lark took her hand and dragged her over to the thigh-highs. Kate looked at the women and asked what they were up to. Both looked shocked that she would think they plotted behind her back and Mrs. Hager explained that they just wanted her to be the envy of every single man in the building. Then they took her to a shoe store and she bought a pair of three-inch heels that according to them matched her dress beautifully.

On the night before the big festival Kate worked. It was late and Harry didn't know why he'd decided to stay open. There'd only been a few customers in the late afternoon, but it was after eight in the evening and the diner stood empty. He told Kate she might as well change into street clothes and stay warm. If someone didn't show up in the next forty minutes he would close at nine. When Kate tried to volunteer to work the next night, Harry explained he only closed three days a year. Christmas day, New Year's Day and the day of the Christmas festival were those days and he told her that most of his customers were home, cooking up things for the party and didn't have time to go out to eat.

She went into the locker room and took off her uniform. She put her jeans on over her white tights and pulled a turtleneck on. She tucked it into her pants and put on a navy blue sweatshirt. She sat down on the bench to put her shoes back on when she saw the door open a little.

"Are you decent?" she heard Harry ask.

"Yep." She smiled as he walked into the room.

"Wouldn't you just know it, we have a customer. You can leave your jeans on; it's

Christmas time, for Pete's sake. I'll get the grill ready." He turned around and went out.

Kate finished her shoes laces and picked up her order pad. She couldn't remember if there was any coffee left in the pot.

She walked down the hall, tied her apron around her waist and stopped dead in her tracks. Jay sat at the counter and looked at the menu. He looked thin and worn-out. Kate took a step back and then moved forward. There was no reason they couldn't be friends.

She grabbed the pot of coffee, which was thankfully half-full, and made her way down to where he sat. She saw his incredible brown eyes glance up and her heart began to stutter in her chest.

"Hi, Jay," she said. "Do you want coffee?"

"Yeah." He turned the cup on the counter over.

She poured the coffee, put the pot down and bent over to retrieve a pitcher of cream from the mini-refrigerator. She couldn't look at him. "What can I get for you?" She wanted to answer, *Me?,* but didn't think this would be a good time to joke around, even if it wasn't a joke.

"Bacon, Swiss cooked medium-well." He put the menu aside and folded his hands on the counter.

She looked up at him. "Do...do you want fries?" she stuttered.

"Yeah."

"Okay." She picked up the pot and put it back onto the warmer and then put Jay's order on the wheel. She kept her back to him and tried to figure out what she hadn't cleaned for the day. She needed to keep busy or she would stare at him and make him uncomfortable while he ate his dinner. She remembered she needed to refill the salt and pepper shakers, grabbed a tray and started to walk around the tables. She collected the shakers and put them onto the tray. When it was full she went to the end of the counter and set it down. She got the big jars of salt and pepper and started to fill the containers. She quickly glanced at him, and saw he just looked straight ahead, over the counter. When she heard the bell from the kitchen ding, she saw Jay's order in the pass-window.

She went up and pulled the plate down. She carefully placed it down in front of him and started to turn.

"Could I get some Ketchup?" he asked.

"Ketchup, right, sorry," she whispered. She got a bottle from under the counter and then went back to the shakers. She glanced at her watch and would recheck his coffee in five minutes.

"I understand you went shopping with my mom," he said and put a French fry into his mouth.

Kate froze for a second and bit the inside of her cheek. "Yeah, she and Lark invited me to go over to Pueblo to the Mall. I have six pairs of pants, a dress and four pairs of shoes now." She continued to pour salt and thought that had to be the dumbest reply she'd ever come up with. Couldn't she think of something just a little more clever to say?

"Did you tell her we'd broken up?"

She put the lid back onto the shaker. "No, she already knew."

"She's read me the riot act a couple of times about it. I told her to mind her own business," he said.

"Oh." Kate opened another shaker and began to pour. She felt surprised by his response to his mother. "Do you want some more coffee?"

"No." He glanced up at her. "Why didn't you press the charges against your mother? Why did you let Frank talk you into all that bullshit?"

"I don't want to see my mother ever again. The deal to be banished from Colorado seemed the best way to get her out of my life. It's finished now. If she comes back, the police will arrest her and the charges will be reinstated. I don't think she'd be that stupid." She didn't want to discuss her mother ever again or think of her. She needed this discussion to change. "Your mom told me about what happened to

Matt, with the bombing and all. I was really sorry to hear about it and I hope he's doing okay. Are they still planning to go to Maryland after the New Year?"

"Yep."

Jay's brother, Matthew, had only another couple weeks left of his tour in the Middle East, when his squad got hit by the insurgents in the area they patrolled. A bomb went off near him and sent several pieces of a truck into his leg. The last Jay's mom told her was that Matt might lose his leg, but it wasn't certain. He'd been flown first to some hospital in Germany than over to the Walter Reed Military Hospital in Bethesda, Maryland. Mr. and Mrs. Hager had already flown back there once and planned to return the first week in January. Mrs. Hager tried very hard to be strong, but Kate could tell the woman worried for her son. It broke Kate's heart.

Jay twirled a fry in the ketchup, but didn't put it into his mouth. "Mom said you were going to help her at the festival tomorrow night."

"I am, yes."

"I'm surprised you're still here. I thought you would have caught a bus by now."

"I decided to wait until spring when the weather's better." She turned and put full shakers down on the closest table. This discussion made her frustrated and angry. She wanted to find a way to forget what happened between them and move on, but he seemed determined to keep pressing her on subjects that hurt her. It was enough and he didn't need to keep it up. She thought about going back into the kitchen and heard him shuffle. She looked down the counter at him.

Jay put his coat on and took his wallet out of his back pocket. He threw a twenty on the counter. "Keep the change," he said with his back to her.

Without looking back, he walked through the front door. Kate looked at his plate and saw it wasn't even half-touched.

"Damn, I should have apologized," she said and thought she should follow him. She'd rehearsed over and over the last few weeks what she wanted to say to him if they ever crossed paths, but, as usual, her mouth and brain weren't on the same wavelength. She could have kicked herself all the way to Mars.

"What?"

Kate looked at the pass-window and saw Harry. "Nothing, I'm just mumbling to myself."

"Where'd Jay go?"

"He left." She went back to the shakers.

Harry came out of the kitchen and looked at the plate. "That's weird. Jay's always been a member of the clean plate club. He barely touched the burger."

"Boss, why don't you head home? I'll finish this up and get the garbage out. Then I'll lock up and go home, too."

"Okay. You don't need to worry about the cans in the kitchen. They're already done. You just need to empty this one. See you tomorrow and save me some of Mrs. Hager's macaroni salad. It's the best, but she won't give me the recipe," he said and patted her shoulder. He handed her the keys. "Oh, don't forget to lock the back door."

"Thanks, Harry. See you tomorrow."

As she finished the shakers, she thought about Jay. Not knowing what to say to him made her feel like an idiot. When she saw him it made the sorrow she'd felt since the meeting with the judge come back full force. She put her hands on the table where she'd just placed the refilled shakers. Her head sank down and she closed her eyes. She willed herself not to cry. She'd done enough of that. She needed to pull up her socks and stop thinking about him. She needed to get on with her life, just like Frank told her to do.

"Yeah, right." She shook her head and straightened up. "Where do I start?" She put more shakers out on the tables. "I'm going to have to get a self-help book," she mumbled. "Oh wait, I have a therapist now at the women's center." She walked back to her locker and got her jacket.

At the counter, she tied up the garbage sack and took it out the back door to put into the big dumpster. She looked down the alley and felt the cold down to her bones. She went back into the diner and locked the door behind her. She grabbed her purse and on her way out, turned off the coffee warmer. At the front door she hit the light switch and turned off the Open sign. She went out the door and locked the deadbolt, then pulled the iron-gate shut and locked it. She put the keys into her pocket and walked to the end of the building.

Turning left, Kate started to cut across the gravel lot, but stopped. Jay's Jeep sat parked about fifty feet from where she stood. He sat under a tall, bright lamp and looked out at her. When her heart started to pound, she couldn't figure out what she should do.

The door to the Jeep opened and Jay got out. He moved to the front and leaned against the bumper.

Kate's first instinct was to run, but she knew the time for fight or flight was now and she decided she needed to fight.

"I know you lied to me because you thought it would protect me from your mom," Jay said and ran his hand over his jaw. "I told you, but you don't seem to remember that people who are close in small towns tend to protect one another. Even if we hadn't told the team's parents, your mom's lies wouldn't have done any good. I grew up and went to school with most of those folks. They never would have believed it."

"First lesson," Kate mumbled and didn't move, but she wanted to run to him and feel the warmth she'd felt so many weeks ago. "I was going to apologize for the lie that night when I woke up in the hospital, but you left. So, I'll say it now. I'm sorry. I know it doesn't mean much anymore, but I am very sorry. It killed me to hurt you."

Jay took a folded piece of paper out of his pocket and opened it. He held it up. "This is the letter you left. I've looked at it every day since my mom found it in the kitchen at my house. You wrote that you love me. I'd rather hear it from your lips than read it."

Kate bit her bottom lip. She felt her throat tighten and knew the flood gates were going to open.

"Jay, I..." her voice cracked and she cleared her throat. "I did...I do love you, very much. I..."

"Is that another lie?" he asked with very little emotion.

"No, it's the truth." Kate felt anger start up the back of her neck. "Jay, I..."

"Truth, yeah right," he said. He put the paper back into his pocket. "Why didn't you run? You were all packed. I saw your bag on your bed and it was all ready. What stopped you from going after you were saved from your mother?"

"I felt tired. That night, in the hospital, Frank said relationships are a two-way street and I was worth fighting for." Tears started to roll down her cheeks. "He said I needed to be willing to fight, too." She pulled a tissue out of her pocket and blew her nose. "I started going to a psychologist a couple of weeks ago at the women's center, because I don't know how to fight for what I want. She's helped me with my running issues, too, and other things. Jay, you're being mean and I am very sorry I hurt you, but if that's all you want to do, then believe me when I say I've kicked myself around the block enough times in the last few weeks and I don't need you to do it to me, too."

"Yeah, I've been angry," he said and frowned. His voice softened. "So, you're working on it? Your issues?"

"Three times a week." She dried her eyes. She tried to figure out what he wanted, but couldn't read the look on his face. It wasn't the anger she'd seen before. He looked tired.

"You haven't been to the rink."

"No, I've stayed away."

"Why?"

"I knew you were angry and I didn't want to make you uncomfortable in your place of business. It wouldn't have been fair to you."

He nodded again and continued to stare at her. A silence fell between them and Kate began to shiver as the cold air worked its way into her bones. She waited, desperate for him to ask another question, but he just watched her.

"Well, I'm frozen, so, I guess I should head home," she said. She didn't know what to say or do to make it right with him. They were at a standoff.

Jay pushed himself away from the Jeep and walked right up to her. Kate felt his hand on her cheek and he moved her face up to look at him. He leaned down, put his lips on hers and his other hand moved around her waist.

Kate's lips parted and she let him devour her. His tongue forced hers back and traced the roof of her mouth and around her teeth. He nibbled her lips and tongue and then sucked on her ear lobe.

When he pulled back, he appeared to be out of breath and put his forehead on hers. Kate felt stunned and grabbed the front of his jacket. She never wanted to let him go.

"My mom said if I didn't learn how to forgive, I'd never find the right woman to share my life with." He opened his eyes and looked into hers. "She hit me on the back of the head and told me I acted like an idiot and needed to think about what all this meant to you. She said I should remember everything you'd been through and how you'd tried to protect me. My dad, on the other hand, said I'd found the right woman and I would lose her forever if I didn't shape up."

"Oh," was all Kate could think to say.

"Some moms and dads can be pretty smart, you know?" He put his hands over hers on the front of his jacket. "Kate, I won't beg you to not run anymore. It sounds good to me that you've gotten some help. I've missed you so much." He put his arms around her and pulled her close.

Kate moved her hands around his waist and felt the warmth she remembered. He kissed her neck and actually bit her.

"Would you want to do a skate around tonight?" he asked, quietly and put his hands into her hair.

"No, not tonight. I got a small Christmas tree and some decorations, but I haven't done anything with it yet." She leaned back and looked up at him. "It's still early. Would you want to help me get it decorated? It's small and shouldn't take very long. I could make a pot of coffee and we could talk. I have a coffee maker now." She pressed her lips together to keep them from trembling.

"I'd like that," he said and turned them toward the Jeep. "New pants, new shoes, a coffee pot and a Christmas tree? You must be rich."

"No, I have a slush fund."

He looked down at her and his eyebrows came together.

"I save all of my tips for a rainy day, which used to be catching a bus or train. Since I've decided not to leave Canon City right now, I've splurged a little. I even got a kitten."

"You're kidding."

"No, I'm very serious. He's a little orange tabby. I call him Ozzie, because he's all mysterious like the wizard."

"What's the dress for?" They stopped at the Jeep.

"Oh, when your mom asked me to help her at the Festival tomorrow night, she informed me that I needed to be dressed nice. All I had were jeans and sweaters."

Jay opened the door of the Jeep. "She did, huh?"

Kate felt something hit her forehead and looked up. "Hey, it's snowing." She held out her hand and caught a flake on her palm.

She watched it start to come down for a minute and then Kate got into the Jeep. Jay leaned in and kissed her again. This time he touched her with less force and more tenderness.

"You know, sweetheart." He kissed the corner of her mouth and sucked on her bottom lip, lightly. "I just may have to dance with you tomorrow night. My mom will have to go it alone for a few minutes. I've only seen you in your work uniform and sneakers. It's a real dress, right?"

They sat on Kate's couch and talked until four o'clock in the morning. The kitten had no fear of Jay and snuggled for a while on his lap, before it retired for the night on her pillow.

Kate told him about the things she and her counselor discussed. Most of it had to do with her fears and her need to run and hide. She explained that there were some things she would have a difficult time getting out of her system, but now that she'd become more aware of the triggers, she would be able to control it better.

Jay told her about what he'd done to the kitchen the day she was in the hospital. Now, he couldn't remember if he'd been that angry with her or if he was pissed at himself for deserting her when she needed him most. He apologized for leaving her that day and hoped she could forgive him.

At four, Jay got off the couch and said he should head home. They both had a lot to think about and should probably get a good night's sleep to do the thinking. Before he opened the door, he turned and pulled her into his arms. She wrapped her arms around his waist and held on to him. It was so good to know that Jay still felt something for her. They'd both steered clear of saying the three simple words and she wanted to, but thought a better time might come down the road, when he trusted her more and wasn't afraid she'd leave without a word.

Jay kissed her and told her to sleep easy and left. She locked the door and stood with her back to it for several minutes. She didn't know if she felt happy or sad that he'd left. She'd wanted him to stay, but felt something swim inside her that she wasn't sure of. It was a thing she'd never felt before and didn't know how to identify it. She hit the light switch and started toward her bedroom and thought she may have just come up with a new topic for her therapist.

Chapter Twenty-Seven

Lark Stone showed up at Kate's door at three o'clock the afternoon of the festival. She carried with her a sack full of hair products. Kate had just gotten out of the shower and was about to start doing her make-up when she heard the knock.

"Hey there," Lark said. "Libby asked me to come over and help you get ready for the party tonight."

Kate opened the door all the way and felt a little stunned. Lark wore jeans and a sweatshirt, but her hair was done up and her make-up looked impeccable. "I just started to get ready. Mr. and Mrs. Hager are picking me up at five o'clock so we can start getting the table ready."

"Two hours is perfect. We'll have plenty of time."

"Plenty of time for what?" Kate asked.

"To get you gorgeous, so Jay will stumble all over himself to impress you." Lark took her hand and led her into the bathroom. "Actually, I'll help with your hair and make-up. You'll have to dress yourself. I have to get home, change into my party dress and help my grandmother load up her pies. I also need to corral my husband, who, if I know him, will be in his office, studying his brains out. Charlie is going to veterinary school and is very dedicated." Lark pointed at the toilet. "Sit."

Kate laughed and sat down. She still wore her towel wrapped around her and her hair continued to drip. She saw Lark look around the bathroom. "Lord, this is small. Where do you keep your towels?"

"I have one and only one and I'm wearing it at the moment." She saw Lark frown. "I have paper towels in the kitchen."

"Those will work. No stay seated. I can get them."

The first thing Lark did was start up Kate's hairdryer and got the drips under control. It still felt a little damp when she stopped, but she said for right now it would be good enough and they could start her make-up.

Lark looked at the few items Kate used and said, "It's a good thing I brought some things with me." She applied foundation and blush, pulled some really pretty eye shadows out of her bag and painted on some eye-liner. Then she very gently applied mascara. "I always do this part very slowly, because I once poked myself in the eye with the brush and was sure I'd been blinded for life. I've never put it on someone else and I'd kill myself if I poked you in the eye. Look up."

Lark fussed and did this and that and finally tilted her head and nodded. "I think I have created a masterpiece."

"Can I look now?" Kate asked. She wanted to see what real make-up looked like on her face. Lark nodded and Kate stood up and looked in the mirror. She barely recognized herself. Her eyelids wore a dark grey-blue shadow that made the blue in her eyes really pop out.

"I didn't realize your eyes were so blue. There's also a little purple in there which is really unusual. For a second I thought you were wearing contacts."

"Jay thought that when we first started to date. I don't see purple, but this make-up color really does make the blue stand out." She continued to look at herself.

"Okay, back down and let's get your hair into a French braid. I think it will look really soft and not as edgy as your pony tail makes you look."

"I'm in your hands, Lark. Thank you so much for doing this."

Lark finished with her hair and took off. As she went out the door she told Kate she expected to hear good news at the party.

Kate looked at the clock and realized she only had half an hour to get dressed. She raced into her bedroom and pulled the thigh-high stockings out of her drawer and managed to get them on without a run. She put on her black lacy panties and the new bra she'd bought, and then slipped her new dress on and zipped it up. She realized her arms were already cold and took the blue sweater out and slipped it on. She looked at herself in the mirror and couldn't believe how good and feminine she felt. Everything came together perfectly and she knew she needed to repay Lark for years to come. She spun around and laughed.

At five o'clock sharp there was a knock on her door and she jumped up from the bed where she'd been putting on her shoes. She grabbed her coat and found Mrs. Hager waiting.

"Oh my god. Kate, you look incredible. I knew Lark would be helpful," Libby said.

Kate saw tears well in her eyes. "No, don't cry. I'm not wearing water proof mascara and I'll only mess everything up."

Libby stood straight and cleared her throat. "Okay, no crying. Let's get moving."

****

The community center was closer to downtown Canon City and cars already started to park in the lot. Kate and Mrs. Hager carried a bag each in and Mr. Hager ferried the rest of the foods in for them. They set up the table and after a few minutes, Kate got a minute to look around. She saw a few people she recognized from the diner and the rink, and then saw Lark over at the beer table. Kate saw the dress Lark wore and was wowed. It was a beautiful form-fitting red dress that came up to her thighs and she moved gracefully in her high heels. Kate thought about it for a minute and then took her sweater off. Her dress wasn't anywhere near as sexy as Lark's, but it would look a damn sight better without the granny sweater.

All of the salads were out and Mrs. Hager put out the cakes, but left them covered. She didn't want them to dry out. A few people started in and made the rounds and the evening began.

Mrs. Hager introduced her to Mrs. Metcalfe and Mrs. Bickens who bickered over their mutual desserts. Mrs. Metcalfe turned out to be Lark's grandmother and seemed like a really sweet lady.

About fifteen minutes after the party started, Charlie Stone walked up to Kate's side of the table and smiled at her and Mrs. Hager. "Good evening, ladies. You both look wonderful this evening."

"Thank you, Charlie. Why are you looking so sneaky?" Mrs. Hager asked.

"Well, I've been hired by your son for a while...or at least until Lark finishes with the beer table. I'm his messenger," he said and took a paper out of his pocket and handed it to Kate.

She opened it and it read - *Hi.* She looked at Charlie. "Okay, what am I supposed to do?"

"You write a reply on the back and I deliver it to my master, blah, blah, blah." Charlie grinned and held out a pen.

"Oh, okay." She took the pen and wrote *hi* back to Jay. She handed the note over to Charlie who walked away. She looked at Mrs. Hager. "That was weird." She laughed.

"My son can be very imaginative when he puts his mind to it."

They were busy for a little while and a line formed from the table as more people began to arrive and the need for food picked up. She'd just served a customer, who picked up their plate and left and Charlie stepped back up to the table. He handed her another slip of paper.

Kate bit her lip and opened it. *You look very beautiful tonight.* She looked around the room, but couldn't see Jay anywhere. "Charlie, where is he?"

"I'm sorry, ma'am. I can't tell you that."

Kate leaned over to write a note back and tried to think of something clever. *Thank you, will I get to see you tonight?* She handed it across to Charlie and watched him move away. She tried to follow where he went, but there were more people who waited for food.

In about fifteen minutes, Charlie stood back in front of her and it caused her to start laughing. *Yes, you'll see me. When you bend over the table I can see the tops of your breasts and it's making me very hot.* Kate felt warmth run up her back and looked at Charlie. "You're not reading these, are you?"

"No ma'am."

Kate thought a minute and then bent over slowly to write the note. She didn't know where Jay was, but wanted to give him a good view. *They're all for you, babe, as is everything else under this dress.* She couldn't help but grin and found it hard to not look around between customers.

At around seven o'clock, Kate heard the DJ start up with the music. She didn't recognize the song, but it was nice enough. She saw Charlie come to the table.

"Just a fair warning, Kate, the gentleman who is courting you this evening has started to sweat. I don't want to speculate whether this is a good thing or if he's come down with the flu. Just so you know, he's started to act a little weird." Charlie smirked and handed her the note.

I want you in my bed tonight and all the nights to come. Every part of your body, heart and soul belongs to me. Woman, you are mine.

Kate read a book once that used the word *swoon* and she finally realized what it felt like. She felt very warm and a tingling started in her pelvis that might drive her mad if Jay didn't show up soon. She almost started to giggle. She looked at Charlie who raised his eyebrows. She picked up a paper bowl and fanned herself.

Finally, she thought of something. *I'm so wet for you, and I think if you touched me with only one finger I might have an orgasm in front of all these people. I love you, Jay and I am yours.*

Earlier in the day, Kate didn't think she'd have a good time at this festival, but the evening turned out to be a complete hoot. She felt happy for the first time in weeks and the thought of being in Jay's arms again made her tingle from head to toe.

Charlie came back quicker this time. He started to hand Kate the note, but pulled it away. "This is the last one. Have a great evening, sweetie." He winked at her and put the note in her hands.

Tell my mother you need to be excused for a while and meet me on the dance floor.

Kate folded the note and held it tight in her hand. She looked at Mrs. Hager who laughed.

"Go on, sweetheart. Jay would never forgive me if I said you couldn't go. I'll get Mike to help me."

Kate turned and headed for the dance floor. When she got closer she saw Jay stood out in the middle. Several couples danced around him and she realized the DJ started a slower song.

Jay looked so handsome; she was going to do that swoon thing again. He wore black jeans that fit very snug on him and a charcoal grey shirt. Over the shirt he had on a black jacket. He watched her take every step.

When she got close, he held out his hand and she walked into his arms. Kate moved her hand up his arm to his neck and his other hand slipped around her waist with his palm on her butt cheek. They started to move side to side and Jay pulled her to him tighter.

Their eyes locked and Kate could feel his hard penis rub against her stomach. She felt a little proud that she may have caused this excitement in him.

Jay leaned over slightly and she could feel his warm breath on her ear. "Just so we're clear, my love, you are mine," he whispered and licked her ear lobe. "I know I wrote it on the note, but I want to make sure you understand how serious I am. No one but me will ever get to touch you. I'm the one you'll wake up with and live life with every day, week and year. I hope this is something you can put up with."

Kate closed her eyes and rubbed her breasts against his chest. She looked up at him and smiled. "I'm all yours, babe, from now until forever." She didn't think it possible, but he somehow managed to pull her closer.

"How long are you supposed to work for my mom tonight? Does she have you signed on for the duration?" he asked.

"No, she said she'd get your dad to help her. I'm free anytime."

He leaned to her ear again. "Babe, I think we should plan on finishing this dance, say goodnight to my folks and then split. If I don't feel your skin soon, tease your nipples with my tongue and take you completely, I may go mad and tear something apart."

Kate's breath caught in her chest and she could only nod.

"Oh and something else." He looked down at her and put his lips on hers, slightly touching her tongue with his. "You don't have to say anything tonight, but would you consider moving in with me and become my wife?"

She pulled back slightly to look into his eyes. Her lips moved, but she couldn't make the words come out.

"It's okay, babe. You don't have to answer me tonight." He put his hand on her neck and started to move in for another kiss.

"Jay, yes."

"Yes?"

"I said it, yes. Now, shut up and kiss me." Kate stood on her toes and mashed her mouth to his. She almost brought her legs up around his waist, but then remembered where they were and thought she'd have to wait.

She came down to her heels, and put her hand on his cheek. "I love you, Jay. You're the only man for me."

He picked her up in a hug and spun her around in a circle. "You're the only partner I'll ever want, Kate, in bed, on the ice, anywhere. I love you, too. And, damn, I'm so happy you're mine."

When he stopped and she opened her eyes, she saw his mom and dad stood on the edge of the dance floor with Lark and Charlie Stone.

She looked up at Jay. "I think our secret might be out." She pointed toward his parents and saw him look.

"Oh, they already know. I must have made one hundred phone calls this morning to get this all arranged. I told Mom and, of course, she told Dad. I think she might have told Lark, because Charlie was on board in a heartbeat."

Kate nodded. "Family and close friends, lesson number one. I'm going to have to get used to that."

"It's really a nice thing, you know. Having people you can count on when the going gets tough," he said and leaned in to kiss her again. "Babe, I don't want to be separated from you anymore. You've become a very necessary part of my sanity."

"I agree with you all the way. I hope you won't mind having a kitten in the house."

"Ozzie? No problem, he's cute." He crinkled his nose. "I suppose when you're pregnant, I'll have to do the pooper scooping?"

"Jay, we haven't talked about kids. How many do you think you want?"

Jay laughed and led them off the dance floor. They told the important people around them the news and Jay's mom started to cry and hugged Kate.

Kate couldn't believe how her life changed in less than twenty-four hours. Yesterday, she continued to exist in her alone world and today she'd been given a whole family and friends who celebrated their engagement. She couldn't believe how blessed she'd been to get off a bus in Canon City.

****

They arrived at Jay's house about an hour after they left the festival. On the way, they stopped at Kate's apartment. She needed a change of clothes and started to unzip her dress, but Jay asked her to wait. He wanted to dance with her some more with her in the dress that wasn't a uniform.

She ran into the apartment, left some food for Ozzie and grabbed a pair of pants, sweatshirt and her sneakers. She got into the Jeep with her arms around her clothes.

On the way to Jay's, he asked her to tell the landlady that she would be moving out that week. He wanted her in his home, by Monday and Kate agreed.

He got them to the house and when Kate walked into the kitchen she frowned. "I thought you said you tore the kitchen to pieces."

Jay took the clothes from her and set them on the table. He then helped her with her jacket and hung it up in the hall closet. He walked up behind her and touched her arm.

"Well, I did. I've been working hard the last couple of weeks to get it back together. My dad helped out. I still need to get the sink back in, but it's almost finished." He watched her walk to the counter and she ran her hands over the new surface. "I decided to resurface the top. Do you like it?"

"Is this granite?"

Jay walked up behind her and put his hands on her waist. "No, it's fake granite, but it looks just like it." He leaned over and ran his tongue up her neck to her ear lobe.

"It's beautiful, Jay," she whispered.

"You're beautiful." He moved a hand up and started to move the zipper on her dress down.

"I thought you wanted to dance more." She looked at him over her shoulder.

Jay had the zipper all the way down and reached around her to undo the belt. He felt his lips curl. "I didn't mean that kind of dancing, babe. I've wanted to take this off you for most of the night." He put his warm hand on her shoulder blade inside the dress and gently moved his fingers around her back. He heard her sigh and moved his hand down her back and inside her panties. He pinched her cheek and held on tight.

He felt Kate lean back and his other hand reached around her. Jay flattened his palm on her stomach and started up to her breasts. When he felt the push up bra, his eyes opened wide. "What the holy hell? That isn't your cute lacy bra." He laughed and turned her around. He felt the bra and grinned like a school boy.

"This is the bra that your mom and Lark said would accentuate my cleavage, which I believe you noticed earlier."

"Yeah, but this thing feels like a Sherman tank. I can't even feel your nips through it."

She looked up at him again. "I guess you'll have to take it off then and, believe me, I'll appreciate it more than you'll ever know. It's hard to breathe."

Jay felt his heart pick up speed and his penis got harder than he thought possible. "Great God," he whispered and bent over to lift her up. "I love you, woman."

He carried her up the stairs and sat her at the foot of his bed. He put his fingers in the arm holes of her dress and started to pull it off her shoulders. She stood back up and it pooled around her feet.

Jay put his hand on her cheek and kissed her. "Babe, how on earth are you breathing? That looks like a torture device." He looked at her from the bra, to her lace panties, and down to the thigh high stockings.

"You know, I said the same thing to your mom and Lark. They said I'd get used to it." She looked at either side of the bra, put her hands on the sides and pushed. "I suppose it could be tighter."

Jay stopped breathing. He couldn't take his eyes off her chest. He put his index finger down the crease and pulled her closer to him. When he finally looked at her beautiful blue-purple eyes, he saw a strange look on her face. "Babe, what's wrong?" He realized he was still in his jacket and started to disrobe while he watched her.

"It's really strange, Jay. It started last night in the parking lot of the diner." She looked up at him. "I've never felt this before and it's a little scary."

"What does it feel like?" He got down to his Jockey shorts and sat down with her on the bed.

"I'm not sure if it's my head or heart, but everything is calm and seems really clear." She looked at him and laced her fingers with his. "That doesn't make any sense."

"Maybe it's one of the cosmic things, you know? Your waves are in the house of Mars and since we're together my waves are crossing over yours from Saturn just perfectly and we're aligned or something."

She looked at him and raised an eyebrow. "I'm not sure what you just said, but sure, okay. I believe anything is possible."

"Can I undo your hair?" he asked and opened the barrette that held the bottom of her braid.

"Lark put a ton of hairspray in it to hold the loose ends in place. It might be a little stiff."

Jay moved his finger through it to loosen the braid. "So beautiful," he whispered and kissed her neck.

He saw Kate close her eyes and moved his hand down to her back. He began to try to open the clasp on her bra. "Did you know Monica dropped her kid off at the grandparents' house and left town?"

"Really? Frank didn't tell me that." Kate still had her eyes closed and moved her hand up his thigh. "Maybe I'll offer to assist Shelby's skating coach. She always drops her swing leg coming out of her jumps. If she stopped that her balance would be much better."

"That would be nice of you to do that. Shelby at least has a chance at a normal life if her mother stays away from her for a long time." Jay felt the clasp pop and started to move the straps down her arms. "Let's get this bullet proof vest off."

Kate opened her eyes and dropped it onto the floor. She lay back on the bed and put one of her arms over her head.

Jay put his hand on her stomach and looked down at her. He was in heaven.

Epilogue

By the next week, Kate was all moved in with Jay. They brought along her Christmas tree and re-decorated it. Ozzie, the kitten, batted at the string of lights and knocked off the few decorations. They joked about Santa Claus passing them by this year since they weren't married yet and held on to one another. Jay didn't feel worried anymore that she would run and just wanted to hold her tight because it felt so good.

Kate relaxed for the first time in her life. There were mornings when they sat at the dining room table and she'd tear up. She explained to Jay that they were happy tears and one day she would probably take everything they felt for one another for granted, but she would try to hold on to the feeling as long as she could.

They set the date for their wedding to be in June. Kate called her dad and told him the date and that he would have to be in Canon City to give her away. He made the reservation before the end of the year and told Kate he couldn't wait to meet her fiancé.

They woke up on Christmas morning and exchanged small presents. She gave him a small gold key to put on his keychain. She told him it belonged to her heart and he could use it as often as he wished. Jay started to laugh and handed her a small box. When she opened it she looked at him and her brows furled together.

"Did you know about the key?" She took a key out of the box and held it up.

"No, I didn't know, but that's only part of the gift. Close your eyes, babe."

She did as he asked and he led her out of the house to the driveway. When they stopped he told her to open them. Sitting next to Jay's blue Jeep, was a red one, the same make and model.

Kate's mouth dropped open. "What? Jay, darling man, I don't know how to drive." She looked up at him.

"That's why you're going to start lessons the first Monday after the New Year. I've already made the arrangements and you'll be all good to go." He smiled down at her and put his arm around her shoulders.

"Are you tired of driving me to work?"

"No, no...I just thought since you're farther out of town now, it would be easier for you to do your girly stuff if you had your own wheels."

She hugged him. "Thank you. Oh my God, I have a car. This is great," she squealed and ran to the side of the Jeep.

After breakfast, they drove to Jay's parents' house to have Christmas dinner. They told his mom and dad that they'd set the date and planned to marry in June. Mrs. Hager hugged Kate, started to cry and welcomed Kate to the family. They were getting ready to open a bottle of champagne, when the phone rang. It was the hospital back east where Jay's brother was taken after the bombing in Afghanistan. The doctor said Matt did very well with the rehab, but for some reason, he got out of bed yesterday and walked away from the hospital. The military police were doing their best to find him, but at present they weren't sure where he'd gone.

It brought the mood down a little in the Hager household and they all agreed to save the champagne until they could celebrate with Matt.

Later, when Kate and Jay were in bed holding one another, she sat up and looked down at him. "Babe, I've been thinking. We may need to put the wedding off a little. I want your brother to be here and I know your mom and dad would be happier if we did."

"That's sweet, but are you sure? We could always do a Justice of the Peace thing and then have a second wedding later."

"No, I don't mind waiting. We're together and your mom and dad seemed so subdued at dinner. I think we can wait until Matt's here with us."

"Whatever you want to do, sweetie. I'm with you all the way."

"Jay, you don't think there is any reason to be worried about Matt? I mean, he wouldn't do anything bad?" She looked down at him.

"No. Mattie's level-headed and he wouldn't do anything to himself. It would kill my mom and dad and he'd never do that." He pulled her back into his arms and held her tight.

Kate started to cry. "Jay, I don't know what to do. I've never dealt with something like this."

"We're together, babe. We'll hold each other up and deal with it day to day. There's nothing to worry about and I'm sure Matt will show up when he's ready." He rolled her onto her back and propped himself up on his elbow. "Hey, there's nothing we can do right now." He wiped the tears off her cheeks. "You know what?"

"What?"

"The fact that you are so worried about someone you've never met, just makes me love you more and more. You have such a big heart." He leaned over and kissed her chest. "I'm the luckiest man on the planet."

"We might have to argue about that, because I feel like I'm the luckiest." She raised her eyebrows and reached for a Kleenex to blow her nose. She threw the tissue aside and put her arms around his neck. "See, there are so many things that make me feel lucky."

"Like what?"

"Hmm...like when I got off the bus here in Canon City and found that apartment that was only two blocks from the rink. And the rink itself was lucky. I never would have met you if the rink wasn't there. So, I think I'm the luckiest."

Jay chuckled. "Okay, I'll give it to you for now. We may have to discuss it more when I've had a little more time to rationally think about it. Right now, I can't be rational, because of where you are positioned. Your body has made my brain turn to mush." He kissed her again and licked along her jaw.

"Mush brain, huh? Maybe this is a good time to get you to agree to something."

"What are you plotting, my woman?"

Her eyebrow arched and she licked her lips. "Oh, just this and that."

"You are being evil and I can't wait to find out what's in the head of yours."

"I love you, Jay."

"You're mine, woman."

ABOUT THE AUTHOR

Lauren Marie lives with her four cats in Western Washington State. She is the author of One Touch at Cob's Bar and Grill - story 3 of the Montana Ranch Series, Love's Touch - Then and Now, Going to Another Place.

Although, she has been focusing her current efforts in the paranormal romance, time-travel and reincarnation genres, she is currently working on continuing the Canon City Series. The first book - Love's Ember's was released fall 2014.

When she isn't pounding the keys, she is an amateur paranormal investigator. She formed her own group in 2006 to hunt ghosts and some unusual experiences have put in an appearance in some of her stories.

Lauren likes to receive feedback. If you want to send her likes and dislikes, you can go to the contact us page on the web-site laurenmariebooks.com or write to her at laurenmariebooks@gmail.com, themenofhallerlake@hotmail.com. or friend her at facebook.com/laurenmariebooks. She does respond to feedback.

21166223R00188

Made in the USA
San Bernardino, CA
08 May 2015